ONE CAME HOME

AMY TIMBERLAKE

ONE CAME HOME

ALFRED A. KNOPF
NEW YORK

THIS IS A BORZOI BOOK PUBLISHED BY ALFRED A. KNOPF

Visit us on the Web! randomhouse.com/kids

Educators and librarians, for a variety of teaching tools, visit us at
RHTeachersLibrarians.com

Library of Congress Cataloging-in-Publication Data
Timberlake, Amy.
One came home / Amy Timberlake. — 1st ed.
p. cm.
Summary: In 1871 Wisconsin, thirteen-year-old Georgia sets out to find her sister Agatha, presumed dead when remains are found wearing the dress she was last seen in, and before the end of the year gains fame as a sharpshooter and foiler of counterfeiters.
ISBN 978-0-375-86925-9 (trade) — ISBN 978-0-375-96925-6 (lib. bdg.) —
ISBN 978-0-375-98934-6 (ebook)
[1. Missing persons—Fiction. 2. Frontier and pioneer life—Wisconsin—Fiction.
3. Sharpshooters—Fiction. 4. Counterfeits and counterfeiting—Fiction.
5. Wisconsin—History—19th century—Fiction.] I. Title.
PZ7.T479One 2012
[Fic]—dc23
2011037095

The text of this book is set in 12-point Bembo.

Printed in the United States of America
January 2013
10   9   8   7   6
First Edition

For Phil

CHAPTER ONE

So it comes to this, I remember thinking on Wednesday, June 7, 1871. The date sticks in my mind because it was the day of my sister's first funeral and I knew it wasn't her last—which is why I left. That's the long and short of it.

But surely, you'd rather hear the long than the short.

At the moment of the above thought, I stood wedged between Ma and Grandfather Bolte. Ma seemed a statue in black except for the movement of her thumb and forefinger over a scrap of blue-green fabric. Grandfather Bolte sighed, adjusting his hands on the hat he held in front of his belly. Seeing the reverend on the other side of that six-foot hole reminded me that I was "sister of the deceased"—a fancy title for someone who stands quietly, holds her tongue, and maintains a mournful attitude. But I could barely stay still. I was not in this situation by choice, and wore a borrowed black dress to boot. The collar clamped to my neck and the tension of the muslin between my shoulder blades suggested that if I let my arms fall to my sides, the dress would rip somewhere in the proximity of my armpits. So there I was, sticking a finger down my collar, holding my arms out from my sides, and the meaner part of me thinking about walking out—surely, enough is enough. But Grandfather Bolte saved me from strangulation. He unbuttoned the top two buttons on that collar, and from somewhere deep in my depths came a patience I didn't know I possessed. I stayed.

Don't misunderstand me—a funeral is a funeral. Though my sister wasn't in that pine box, a body lay in it sure enough. *Remember,* I told myself many times during the reverend's eulogy, and then as people started shoveling dirt into the hole, *that coffined body down there is dead.* That's a *d* at the beginning and a *d* at the end. There's no forward or backward from "dead," and no breath either—"dead" stops a person cold. It does not make that body your sister, but it is sad, sad news.

The way I figured it, I'd survive this funeral, and then I was free to go.

My sister, Agatha Burkhardt, had run off with pigeoners—two men and one woman in a forlorn-looking buckboard. Sheriff McCabe went after those pigeon hunters, following them all the way to Dog Hollow. One week later he came back with a body.

2

Ma said I was old enough to face facts. So I went with Ma and Grandfather Bolte out to the McCabe stables to "identify."

You could smell the body from outside the building.

Inside, dust hung in a twist of sunlight, an old mare stamped in a far stall, and a pine box lay on a roughly hewn table. Grandfather Bolte walked straight up to that box and slid the lid off.

I do not want to talk about what I saw. But if you're to understand the rest, here's what you need to know: There wasn't a lot of body left (the sheriff said that it'd been exposed to animals). There wasn't a face. There wasn't a left or right hand. The body was wrapped in fabric from Agatha's blue-green ball gown. There was a clump of auburn hair. I started to shake. I still have nightmares (that body was in an advanced state of decomposition). But I am glad I looked. I know what I saw. I also know what I *didn't* see.

Grandfather Bolte put his hand to his mouth and turned away. Ma stood there, taking it all in, pausing for what seemed like months. Then she asked Sheriff McCabe for his knife. When he didn't give it to her, she laid her eyes on him. They stared at each other for a long while, and then he pulled it from its sheath.

It was a big knife—the kind of knife with a sharp, upturned point. Ma took it, reached into that pine box, and sawed a hunk of something off.

I inhaled sharply, not knowing what she was doing.

Then her hands reappeared: the right held the knife, and

the left, a fistful of blue-green cloth. I saw pleats. Ma stepped back.

"You were tracking the pigeoners when you found this?" Ma jabbed the air with the knife.

We knew he was, so the jerk of the knife panicked me a little. Grandfather Bolte tried to reach for the knife, but Sheriff McCabe held him back.

"I was on their trail," the sheriff said.

"She still traveling with them?"

"Pretty sure she was."

"She was shot? In the *face*?" The blade jerked upward.

The sheriff nodded ever so slightly. "I am so sorry, Dora." He laid out the syllables of her name with the most tender care.

Sometimes I forget how long they've known each other.

Ma's chest rose in a long breath. Then she opened up her left hand and nodded at the fabric as it unrolled. "These are my stitches," she said. The knife dropped from her hand, planting itself in the earthen floor. "It's Agatha. We'll bury her tomorrow."

The first minutes of the ride home I kept silent, but the words "bury her" compelled me to speak. I leaned over Ma, who sat in the middle of the buckboard, to speak directly to Grandfather Bolte. "There wasn't enough of the body to be sure—altogether that body couldn't have weighed more than two cats. You've got to go. You'll find her. You should have gone in the first place."

It was bold of me to speak so, but it was commonly known that no one tracked better than my grandfather. (Sheriff McCabe would tell you straight out that he was better at keeping the peace than tracking.) Grandfather Bolte hadn't gone because with the pigeoners in town, our general store had been chaotic and we had been hard-pressed for help. At that point in time, Grandfather Bolte had already spent a couple of days away from the store, and if truth be told, he never thought Agatha's *life* was at risk. Therefore, when the sheriff offered to chase her, Grandfather Bolte took him up on it.

That was a mistake in need of rectification.

I reached over Ma, who'd visibly stiffened, to grab hold of Grandfather Bolte's forearm. "You have to go find her. Please, Grandfather, *please.*"

When I didn't release his forearm, Grandfather Bolte put his hand on top of mine and squeezed.

"You are thirteen years. You'll hold your tongue."

He pointed at me. "We are *blessed* to have a body at all. Now, we are done talking about this. You shut your mouth or you walk home."

Then he looked forward and flicked the reins.

I sat back in a state of shock. How could Grandfather Bolte be satisfied with what we'd seen in that pine box? I understood about Ma. When Pa left in search of Colorado gold, he wrote two letters. These came in the first six months. After that? No word at all. That was ten years ago. Pa had to be dead, but were we certain? No. Ma never did put on mourning black. It was only in the last year that Ma had re-moved her wedding band. So for Ma to have parts of a body wrapped in a blue-green cloth containing her stitches? Well, Ma would think Agatha was dead.

But Grandfather Bolte knew better. Had he forgotten how he taught Agatha to walk silently through a forest car-peted with leaves? Had he lost all recollection of how Ag-atha could read a hillside for the caves it contained? My sister climbed trees as easily as a raccoon. And there was no one better at sneaking off. I thought of all those nights Agatha slipped out of our bedroom. One morning I awoke beside Agatha and saw a fragment of dried leaf in her hair, and that was how I found out she'd been gone.

My sister would never *die* and then *lie* there. It made no sense.

I jumped off the wagon. Going that fast, I tumbled.

"Georgie!" Ma said.

But Grandfather Bolte didn't halt the horses, and Ma didn't tell him to stop.

When I got home, the planning for my sister's funeral was well under way.

It doesn't take long to bury a body when there's need. At ten o'clock the next day, the body was in the hole, and Grand-father Bolte, Ma, and I stood listening to a eulogy by Rev-erend Leland. No headstone—that'd come later. And despite the short notice, there was no lack of mourners—over fifty,

I'd guess. But then again, there's nothing like a sheriff returning to town with a body to spread news of a coming funeral.

Graveside, I noted that Sheriff McCabe came early and stood next to Ma. The other sight worth seeing was Billy McCabe and Mr. Benjamin Olmstead—the two rivals for Agatha's affection—standing so near to one another. Only the four younger McCabe boys separated them. How could they be so civil after all that had happened? Mr. Olmstead was my sister's most recent attachment. Billy McCabe was Agatha's intended: the one everyone thought Agatha would marry.

I remembered the day I'd seen the kiss. That kiss had led to the end of everything. I was glancing out the window in Grandfather Bolte's study as I worked on the daily accounts when I saw it. At the time, my sister was keeping company with Mr. Olmstead, so I gaped as Billy's hand reached for Agatha's chin, guiding her close enough so that his lips touched hers. They drew apart. Agatha said something. She squeezed Billy's forearm, and then she left the sight line of my window. Billy smiled for a moment. Then he put a fist in the air and whooped. And as he left, he whistled. Everything about the way Billy McCabe moved—the way he stuck his hands in his pockets, the little dance step in his feet—told me he'd gained something significant. He'd won either half the world or Agatha's heart. Since Agatha didn't have half the world to give, she'd given her heart.

I told Mr. Olmstead, thinking he had a right to know.

At the funeral, I looked at each suitor, comparing the two of them. Mr. Olmstead owned the Olmstead Hotel. He had thirty-five years of living behind him and silk lapels crisp enough to cut butter. But Billy McCabe was considered the good-looking one. I granted Billy this: he stood half a head taller than Mr. Olmstead. As he'd aged into his nineteen years, his chest and arms had thickened so much I couldn't call him Beanstalk anymore, and his hair had changed from corn-silk white to the color of wet sand. But those characteristics didn't seem enough to warrant the way his grin caused chaos with every idiot girl I'd ever met.

Today tears ran down Billy's face. What I wanted to know was this: Did he grieve because my sister was dead? Or did he grieve because something he'd been *promised* could no longer occur? He had walked off *whistling*.

Polly Barfod, a girl with thick blond braids wrapped around her head, kept her place beside Billy. She was deter-mined to marry him, then. People described her as "sturdy." I stared at her ankles, noted the way the laces stretched tight between shoe leather that did not touch, and thought of the way tree trunks come straight up out of the ground.

But who cared? This entire funeral was lunacy! Within a period of two weeks, Agatha had run off, a body was found, and a funeral was held. Does this strike you as reasonable? I refused to believe it.

I tried to calm myself by focusing my eyes and thoughts on the Wisconsin River, a ribbon of which was visible beyond

Reverend Leland. I noted the location of all that I knew to be there: the sandstone that lined the banks and piled yellow, tan, and red, like giant pancake stacks; the cave that summer visitors carved their names into; the teapot islands with pine-tree lids; and the spires that balanced rocks at their points.

Reverend Leland paused from his sermonizing to read a psalm:

> *The heavens declare the glory of God;*
> *and the firmament sheweth his handywork.*
> *Day unto day uttereth speech,*
> *and night unto night sheweth knowledge.*
> *There is no speech nor language,*
> *where their voice is not heard.*

Psalm 19. My sister's favorite. Reading it was going one too far, given the circumstances. To the psalm's meter, I kicked a trough in the dirt.

Finally, Reverend Leland stopped his eulogy, men returned hats to their heads, and the shoveling began. One by one, the mourners wrapped their hands around the shovel's handle, stuck it into dirt, and dropped the dirt into that six-foot hole. Then they passed the shovel back and came to give their condolences to the family.

Grandfather Bolte spoke with the men, patted a back, and even, at times, laughed. The women headed for Ma. Ma nodded, took a hand. I slid out of arm's reach and listened to that dirt falling into the hole. At first, the rocks had skidded on top of hard wood, but now all I heard was hollow thumps.

When I finally looked up, I saw Ma's left thumb and fore-finger circling on that scrap of blue-green fabric: circle, circle, stop to talk, circle, circle, circle, stop to talk, circle . . .

It reminded me of *that* day. . . .

CHAPTER TWO

Agatha spinning. I couldn't help but think it, seeing Ma's thumb and forefinger working in circles on that blue-green scrap.

Hold it, I thought. I did not want to think about *that*—not here, not now. In front of all these people? I felt their funeral eyes on me, waiting to see how I took my grief. I looked again beyond Reverend Leland at the winding Wisconsin River below and hoped for distraction.

But all that sky between bluff and river did not help. How *empty* the Psalm 19 firmament appeared! Only a couple of weeks earlier, someone standing in this spot would have seen flocks of wild pigeons flashing through the blue sky like schools of fish. Those pigeons were gone. They'd left their nesting for good—the nesting had broke—right before Agatha ran off.

Suddenly I was remembering that day whether I wanted to or not.

That was the day the world darkened under wild pigeons. It was the end of March. Mrs. Finister had rushed into our store all out of breath.

"Pigeons," she said to Ma, throwing herself against the counter. "They're coming. I never saw so many."

Ma raced out back to gather laundry hanging on the line. Agatha bolted upstairs. Mrs. Finister stepped toward the plate glass window. I pushed past Mrs. Finister out onto the front porch.

People from Wisconsin know wild pigeons. Pigeons come every year, but because 1871 was an odd-numbered year, we were expecting greater numbers: pigeons adore black-oak acorns, and black oaks drop acorns every *other* year. So to put it plainly, Mrs. Finister's agitation must have meant she'd seen something unusual.

But outside, from my position on the porch, Placid, Wisconsin, looked as it always did: There was Main Street (bakery, blacksmith, three inns, tailor, photographic studio, courthouse, church, and train depot). The March sky held its place above, with melting snow and mud below.

Something didn't seem right, though. I figured it out— there was a sound on the air, a shushing. The wind was brisk, so at first I thought it was the wind. But wind lets up—it's not constant—and there was no letup to this sound. It was like a teakettle when the water boils and steam plumes out the spout. Then the shushing grew louder—more like a steamboat powering itself upstream. No—make it two or three steamboats and a couple of trains headed right for me.

Fear took me. My knees began to knock—and I mean that literally. My body soon followed suit. Then my ears stopped up and all I heard was the shushing, shushing, shushing. This convinced me of oncoming catastrophe: somehow I was sure that a wall of water rushed at the porch I stood on. I gripped the railing, unable to move my feet from where they'd anchored. I swear I was Noah awaiting his flood.

I saw them then—pigeons, not water. But whatever relief I felt at seeing birds, it dissipated when that winged mass drew a shade on the sun. I tell you, it was night at three o'clock in the afternoon. My world snapped into a box. The air staled. A kind of sleet (the birds' dung) fell from that winged ceiling.

Birds, birds, birds—a wing, an eye, a beak—they flew so fast I couldn't pick out one bird. The sky was a feathered fabric weaving itself in and out, unraveling before my eyes. I felt dizzy. I could barely breathe.

Out on the street, people dropped to the ground, arms thrown over their heads. If they screamed, I wouldn't have known, because all I could hear was the sound of those beating wings. Horses reared up and yanked at their hitches. Dogs flattened their ears, put their heads down, and scooted under buggies and porches.

Then Agatha brushed my elbow, startling me. She had

changed into her oldest dress and covered it with her work apron. Oddly, she carried Ma's tattered parasol.

She winked at me, popped open the parasol, and stepped off the porch.

I reached out to stop her because I thought she'd get hurt, but Agatha was already beyond my grasp. Wild pigeons are as big as crows. They fly fast and with much strength. They'll knock you off your feet and cause all sorts of damage.

Agatha, though, seemed to feel no fear. A current of pigeons flew low in the street before veering up over the roof of our store. Agatha ran toward this winged river, stopping short of collision by mere inches. Then she crouched down and edged underneath it.

Bit by bit, Agatha lifted the parasol, forcing the rush of pigeons to adjust. Finally, she stood upright under a flood of birds that surged over and around, without stop, repeatedly and repeatedly, again and again, to infinity (it seemed). Agatha beamed at me and pointed.

But even that triumph was not enough for Agatha, because then she spun. At first, she spun slowly, carefully. But soon she turned quicker, more swiftly still, until the fringe on the parasol shot out parallel to the ground. The pigeons pivoted, point-turning near Agatha's right cheek—one after another after another. Locks of Agatha's auburn hair came undone and lifted off her shoulders.

Have you ever seen how iron filings circle a magnet? That was what this looked like. Except it wasn't still and dead like iron; it was rushing, pulsing, and made of feathers, pumping hearts, and lungfuls of air. I could barely make out the pigeons, but I could see the center: my sister turning and laughing under that parasol. My fear slipped to the wayside, and I felt something like what I feel when I hear bells on horses, or streams running during the first spring thaw. I couldn't take my eyes off her. Agatha—sister, friend, guide to life, and the eighth wonder of my world.

As if she heard my thoughts, Agatha stopped and pointed at me. "Come," she mouthed. Her free hand gestured me closer. She nodded encouragingly.

I wanted to. I did. I tried to pull my fingers from that railing, to instruct my feet to lift and step. But those images of bells and streams dissolved, and all I saw was a wind stirred by the evil winged creatures from Pandora's box. I stayed.

At the funeral, it was the memory of my refusal that made me cry. My arms pressed to my sides, the fabric of that borrowed black dress ripping under my armpits, the sound so loud I'm sure people heard it above the shoveling.

When Grandfather Bolte put his large hand on my shoulder, I shoved him away and ran down the long hill from Mount Zion Cemetery.

CHAPTER THREE

I ended up sitting in my oldest clothes down by the river, shooting gin bottles to pieces with the Springfield single-shot. Gin shacks had sprouted along the river with the influx of the pigeoners that followed wild pigeons. Now that the people had left, bottles littered the bank. I found those bottles convenient. Shooting settled me. I did not miss one bottle. I never do.

Feathers flew up with each breaking bottle. Pigeon feathers that spring were like fallen leaves in the autumn—they were everywhere, *in* everything. But there's a difference between feathers and leaves. Feathers claw their way back into the sky, whereas leaves, after flying once, are content to rest on the earth. Agatha? She was a feather. She pushed higher, farther always. I suspected my constitution was more leaf than feather. I hoped I was wrong about that, though, because I wanted to be like Agatha.

Wherever she was. And I *would* find her.

I lifted the rifle, took aim, and shot another bottle to smithereens.

The blank side of a used store receipt lay beside me (weighted down with an old brick). I'd written "For Journey" at the top and underlined it. But my mind was elsewhere. Memories pressed in on me, so I had set the pencil down and picked up the Springfield rifle.

The first thing I remembered was the fight in November. I heard Agatha's raised voice, and then Grandfather Bolte's coming from the proximity of his study. By this time I was in our bedroom, tucked in bed and, because of the cold, eagerly awaiting Agatha's warm body beside me.

Though I tried to hear, I couldn't make out a word of the fight. Ma stepped into the hallway, knocked on the study door, and called their names. Hinges creaked. Ma and Agatha spoke. "Ask *him*," I heard Agatha say. Next thing I knew, Agatha was in our room and closing the door behind her.

She spoke rapidly. Agatha told me she'd asked for tuition money for the University of Wisconsin at Madison as her Christmas present. She explained how she had offered to spend her savings, which she said was enough for the first year's tuition. But still, Grandfather Bolte had turned her down flat, saying the only thing she'd get at the university was a *husband,* and *that* could be found in Placid, Wisconsin, for *free.*

She wouldn't answer any of my questions. Instead, she lay down. I knew she wasn't asleep—she was gripping her pillow like it was a log saving her from submersion.

When I was sure she wouldn't say more, I lay back upset. It was no surprise that Agatha wanted to study the natural sciences, but I'd never thought that meant more than reading books and rambling through the woods to observe and sketch. I'd never considered that she'd want to learn from a teacher, or to formalize it with an official piece of paper. It was a lot of effort, and for what? It would not lead to work. Grandfather Bolte was right.

That she had enough money to go to university for one year was another thing altogether. Agatha was good at making money. She gave tours to ladies wanting to explore the river and its caves, and she sold seeds and seedlings in our store. But I had no idea she'd saved up so much money. Was it *all* in that tin box under the closet floorboard? I had never dared to look. The one time I happened to *step* on that particular board (and I swear that's all I did), Agatha questioned me for an hour.

No, I was not in favor of Agatha's going to university, because it meant Agatha would leave Placid and me. Happily, Agatha did not speak of going again. I thought her craving for education was cured.

★ ★ ★

On Christmas Day, Grandfather Bolte gave me a present that made me yelp happily and hang on his neck. He told me I could take whatever ammunition I needed from the store as long as I showed him what I shot. Agatha wasn't so lucky. Her present was a set of embroidery hoops, small to large. I do not know how she did it, but Agatha acted genuinely thankful.

Then Ma gave Agatha the blue-green ball gown, and everything passed away in the presence of that lovely, lovely gown. The color in that silk was so subtle and shifting we carried the dress all around the house to see it in different light. "You can wear it at the New Year's ball," Ma said.

Agatha did wear it to the Olmstead Hotel New Year's ball. She made turn after turn around the ballroom in Billy McCabe's arms while wearing that dress. Agatha's auburn hair shimmered, and the crystal from the chandelier flecked Billy and Agatha in light. And that dress? The blue-green color caught your eye the way a hummingbird does: flicking in front of you, capturing your attention, then—suddenly— disappearing. As I watched Agatha spin around the ballroom, I heard my neighbors bet that by the end of January, Agatha Burkhardt would be engaged to marry Billy McCabe. I hated that idea. Marrying Billy was worse than attending the University of Wisconsin because Billy planned to homestead in Minnesota. Minnesota was so far away Agatha might never come home again.

★ ★ ★

Perhaps Billy asked her, I thought as I loaded ammunition into the Springfield. *But if he did, she must have said no. There were no engagements announced in January.* I lined up the rifle, pulled the trigger, and nailed the brown bottle directly in the middle of the label. It disintegrated.

I loaded another cartridge, took aim, and shot. I repeated the process again and again. Every once in a while, I imagined mourners gathering in our home, asking after me. I was glad to be far away, sitting by the river with a rifle nestled in my shoulder. One by one, I let the bright, crisp sound of shattering bottles clear my head.

I shot the last bottle, set the gun down, and went to line more up.

As I sat on my stump, I noticed my list. It said "For Journey" and nothing else. I picked up the pencil and wrote the one thing I knew I needed. Then I let the pencil drop and laid my hand on the rifle.

While I fired at bottles, the last good conversation I'd had with Agatha came to mind. It was the middle of May. This was after I'd seen her kiss Billy and ten days before she left. In light of what happened later, the conversation seemed rife with portent, but I did not see it then.

Agatha had been giving me the silent treatment for my big mouth, but that night:

"Georgie?"

Agatha's voice. I pivoted to see.

Agatha smiled. She patted the bed. I knew what that

meant, even though she hadn't done it since I was eight or so. I jumped into the center and arranged myself cross-legged. She climbed up and kneeled behind me. She undid my braids. Then she rested one hand on the crown of my head and used the other to drag a brush through my hair. Tingling ran through my body. I closed my eyes. It was going to be all right now. She'd forgiven me. I knew it.

"There was once a wise old man who lived by himself in a forest lodge . . . ," Agatha began.

In my mind, tree trunks lined up side by side and branches wove into a roof.

"In the afternoons, the man liked to sit and think. He thought about everything—animals, trees, birds, insects, plants, and people. He thought about how things worked, and why things happened, and where each living creature belonged in this world. Because he spent so much time thinking, he became the wisest person in his village. . . ."

"This is a story about you," I crowed. Agatha never could tell a story that wasn't somehow about herself, and Agatha *could* go on and on about the natural world.

Agatha tugged harder on the brush. "It's from the Seneca. Most of it, anyway."

I pretended I hadn't said a thing and sat stock-still. The brush resumed its slow descent through my hair.

"One afternoon, as this man sat thinking, a white pigeon flew into his lodge and landed on the man's stool. Now, this was no ordinary pigeon. Instead, it was a messenger sent from another people, much greater than the wise old man and those in his village. The old man watched the pigeon, waiting. The white pigeon blinked at him with one eye, twitched, blinked at him with the other eye, and then spoke: 'As a token of respect, the Council of Birds has decided to give a gift from my kind, the pigeons. Each spring, man will seek the wild pigeons. They will take some of the young and leave the adults. In summer, fall, and winter, man will leave the pigeons alone.'

"The wise old man bowed and then rushed out of his lodge to tell the people. When he returned, the white pigeon was gone, except for one white feather that rested in the middle of the floor. The old man picked it up and studied it. As he did so, he saw another feather near a window ledge. He walked to that feather and picked it up, and saw a feather just outside. And so the wise old man walked from one feather to the next right out of his village. Feather by feather he picked out his path."

Agatha paused.

I turned around and blurted what I'd been thinking: "When we own the store, you can leave anytime. You can do your studying. You'll have to check with me to make sure I've got help, but after that you can leave. I won't stop you."

My intention was to show her how bighearted, how magnanimous, I'd become. Yes, I'd told Mr. Olmstead, and perhaps I did feel bad about doing it, but it was for the best.

She'd spoken to me and brushed my hair; I thought I was giving something back.

Agatha pulled my hair into a braid—roughly.

"Ouch!" I put my hand to the back of my head.

"Nice of you to *let* me study. Maybe I wanted to get married to Mr. Olmstead." She tied off the braid and let it fall against my back.

"Then you shouldn't have kissed Billy McCabe!" The words sprung from my lips.

Agatha's face reddened. "You should have talked to me first. Not gone straight to Mr. Olmstead."

"It was the *right* thing to do," I said.

She smacked the mattress once, hard. "Hair done. Time for bed."

"Agatha!" I said. But, as ordered, I got under the covers. Agatha joined me—wordlessly, of course.

There was a long pause, then Agatha sighed and turned to face me. She grabbed my hand. "Listen to me, Georgie. I love you. No matter where I am, or what I'm doing, I always love you."

I blinked, confused. "I know. I love you too."

Agatha squeezed my hand and began to roll over. But before she turned away from me, I started in: "It won't be so bad. . . . A living is as good an inheritance as anyone's got. I'd make a fine partner."

Agatha groaned. "All you do is parrot Grandfather Bolte. I'm going to sleep."

"You'd be a *full* partner. I'm making you an offer. More than equitable too, given how much you like to wander off."

"You're thirteen years old . . . ," said Agatha, moaning. She wrapped her head in her pillow.

I leaned over her padded head and spoke to her nose. "I did the work of an eighteen-year-old *and* a thirteen-year-old while you were busy with Mr. Olmstead." The entire situation made me want to spit.

"My sister, Georgie, worked so, so hard. Let's go to sleep," said Agatha. She grabbed at the covers and yanked them up under her chin.

"I had to scrub that porch of pigeon droppings. And stock every other item. *And* help with the customers. Ma and Grandfather Bolte wore me out for you."

At this, Agatha huffed. "You liked it. You *love* that store. You are a store owner through and through. And I've never seen anyone take to numbers like you do," she said.

"What's wrong with liking numbers? I've got a head for them. Which means maybe I shouldn't be spending all day scrubbing defecation off pine boards! You should have seen my knees. Cracked up like the Sahairy Desert. It wasn't fair," I said.

Agatha laughed. "What desert? Say it again."

"Sahairy Desert," I said.

"Sa-har-a," she said.

"It looks like 'hairy' in the books."

"Does not!" she said.

"If you read it fast enough, it does! Anyway, you *understood* what I meant. You just made me say it so you could look well-read. That's prideful," I said. I couldn't maintain anger, though. There was Agatha grinning at me. I fought a smile, lost, and grinned back.

"They would have made you scrub lime no matter," said Agatha.

"Maybe. A deal? Spinsters? Together?" I held out a hand.

"You never give up."

She did not take my hand. But all was well. "Glad you're staying," I said.

"I know," she said.

"What did you say to Billy that day? He looked so pleased with himself. He whistled and whooped. . . ."

"Georgie, shhh," she said, and rolled over.

"Please," I said to her back.

"Good. Night."

She would not tell me more. I rested my feet against Agatha's calves. She didn't resist the cold of my toes. And like that—my feet on her calves—I closed my eyes. I thought, *From here on out, the situation can only get better.*

Of course, it did not get better.

Ten days after telling the story of the white pigeon, my sister, Agatha, ran off. The date was Thursday, May 25. If the pigeons left with a great clapping sound, my sister slipped off with no sound at all.

My family lived in ignorance for at least two days, mostly due to what we knew of Agatha's character. On Thursday, we thought Agatha had gone on a walk after running that blacksmith's errand she'd mentioned. On Friday morning, when Agatha hadn't returned or slept in her bed, we thought she had spent the night in one of those caves on the Wisconsin River. Though it did not excuse the behavior (chastisement awaited), she'd done this sort of thing before, and Agatha had experienced the hardship of a broken attachment with Mr. Olmstead. Being outdoors was the only thing that made Agatha feel better.

Saturday—the third day—worry set in. These worries centered on mishaps: losing her way (unlikely), twisting her ankle (possible), getting stuck in a cave (plausible). Grandfather Bolte and Sheriff McCabe set out to search Agatha's haunts. They searched that day and the next (Sunday).

It was on Monday that thoughts of the tin box under the closet floorboard began to beleaguer me. If Agatha found I'd touched it, I'd be in trouble. But it was the only way I'd know, and I didn't think anybody else knew the location of Agatha's savings. After a silent and solemn lunch with Ma, I opened Agatha's closet and pried up the floorboard. As soon as I touched the tin, I knew. The tin rested too lightly in my hand.

I went straight to Ma. "Her money was in this. She's run away." I held out the empty tin.

Ma's glance ricocheted off the bottom of the tin and

landed on me. "Do you have *any* idea where she might have gone?"

Unexpectedly, I did. "Madison? The university? She was saving for tuition."

"Yes," Ma said.

Ma and I quickly searched the whole house to see what else was missing. Both Ma's carpetbag and the blue-green dress were gone from the back closet. Then Ma sent me off to see the stationmaster. If Agatha had boarded a train to Madison, he would know. But the stationmaster claimed he had not seen my sister board any of the trains leaving town. Still, a lot of people were leaving town now that the pigeons had left, and Ma and I thought it possible that Agatha had escaped the stationmaster's notice.

Then Grandfather Bolte and the sheriff returned with news. That Monday afternoon Grandfather Bolte had run across an itinerant field hand who said he'd seen Agatha go off with three pigeoners, a married couple and a single man, in a wobbly buckboard. As far as the field hand knew, they had headed southeast toward Prairie du Chien. Prairie du Chien was not in the direction of the University of Wisconsin at Madison. In fact, it was west of Madison by at least one hundred miles.

On the sixth day—Tuesday, May 30—Sheriff McCabe pursued these pigeoners. He ended up in Dog Hollow, Wisconsin. One week later, on Tuesday, June 6, Sheriff McCabe returned to Placid with a body.

★　★　★

I shot the last bottle and set the gun down. I picked up a pigeon feather, ran my thumb across the edge, and thought of the story of the wise old man and the white pigeon. "Feather by feather he picked out his path," Agatha had said.

I *knew* she was alive.

I looked at my list. Underneath "For Journey" I read the word "horse."

Where the devil was I going to get a horse?

CHAPTER FOUR

As the sun set, I shinnied up the oak tree outside our bedroom, opened the window, and stepped inside. By the time Ma came to say good night, I was well into my act of pretending sleep on my side of the bed.

She stood in the doorway for a long while. I clamped my eyelids shut and tried to regulate my breathing. I'm fairly certain I did not fool Ma.

Yet I would not open my eyes. If Ma had only wanted an apology for causing a scene at the funeral, I might have yielded. But she wanted me to voice my sorrow. She wanted me to say my sister was dead, deceased, perished, passed on. I would say no such thing.

The door shut.

★　★　★

In the middle of the night, I got out of bed. I stumbled to the desk, turned the key on the kerosene lamp, and pulled the store receipt (my list) out of the drawer.

My pen hovered above the paper for a moment or two, and then I set it down. What did I know about travel? I'd never traveled more than a day's journey, and that was sitting next to Grandfather Bolte, with him holding the reins. I'd only been to one town other than Placid. Of course, I'd sold to people who traveled, so I had a few ideas. But people who travel often take fanciful items. I've heard of grand hall mirrors spoken of as necessities, and who in their right mind would *need* that?

I wrote down "food." But what kind of food? I needed to do better than this or I'd never leave Placid.

I recollected something that might help. I opened my bedroom door and crept down the hall. I found the book on the parlor shelf: *The Prairie Traveler: A Hand-Book for Overland Expeditions,* written by Randolph B. Marcy, a captain of the U.S. Army.

I hadn't been that interested in the book before, but now? I figured if this book could get a person to Fort Wallah Wallah and back, it could get me to the spot that body was found—to Dog Hollow, Wisconsin. I would, as the book suggested, "avail myself of its wisdom," and I expected the promised result (inserting myself into Captain Marcy's prose): "Georgie Burkhardt will feel herself a master spirit in the wilderness she traverses."

I snuck back into my room, closed the door, laid the book out on the desk, and began my list in earnest. For food, Captain Marcy suggested bacon packed in bran (to prevent the fat from melting), flour, boiled butter, sugar, desiccated vegetables, and tea. But that was for a much longer journey. If I got a horse, I'd only be gone about a week and therefore could pack perishables—chicken eggs, for instance.

Along with a change of clothing, Captain Marcy recommended packing large colored handkerchiefs; a bar of castile soap for washing the body, and another for washing clothes; a belt knife and a whetstone for sharpening the knife; and a buckskin pouch filled with "stout linen thread, large needles, a bit of beeswax, a few buttons, paper of pins, and a thimble." That seemed good advice even for a journey of short duration.

My plan was to take what we sold in the store. Now, I knew that was stealing. Let's not beat around the bush about what God thinks of taking without asking. But I'd mitigate the hurt by admitting to it. I'd write out an IOU and leave it in the account book. I was sure that after I returned with Agatha in tow, Ma and Grandfather Bolte would understand the situation's urgency.

As for particular clothing, I decided to wear my split skirt. I planned on traveling by horseback, and sidesaddles seemed precarious. Doesn't a person have more chance of staying on top of a horse with one leg over each side? I didn't want to *perch;* I wanted to *clamp.* Not that I'd ridden a horse before, but some things make sense.

31

I'd bring the photograph of Agatha that was on the downstairs mantel. Seeing it might jar someone's memory. And I would take the Springfield single-shot too. I felt some guilt since it had not been given to me outright. But that gun was more or less mine. Grandfather Bolte used the double-barrel. I was the one that hunted with the Springfield.

I put the pen back in its holder and read over my list. Pride welled up until I considered that word "horse" written under "For Journey." I knew it was *possible* to walk to Dog Hollow, but it would take much longer, and it hardly bears mentioning that a thirteen-year-old girl traveling alone might attract attention. The faster I got to Dog Hollow and back, the better.

Where was I going to get a horse?

I couldn't fathom taking one of the delivery-wagon horses. If I did, Grandfather Bolte would be mad enough to eat snakes, and I wanted to come home again. And do not even mention horse thieving as an option—there's theft and then there's horse thieving. Not only does a crime like that stain a family's good name now and forever, there's the Anti–Horse Thieving Society to consider. I swear those men rise out of the river mist when they hear of horse thieving. They trail that thief until caught and don't usually wait for the law to execute justice, tending to leave that thief dangling between broad limb and bare ground.

That left only one place to go: I'd have to get a horse from Billy McCabe. Though I didn't care much for Billy, the McCabes raised horses. In addition, the way our families spent time together made us practically related. What was more, I'd seen Billy cry at that funeral. Seemed to me, he still loved Agatha. (No matter his matrimonial promises to Polly.) There had to be a horse Billy could spare Agatha's little sister.

Fortunately, the very next day Ma needed an errand run in the direction of the McCabes'. I wasted no time getting to the McCabe ranch.

I heard the scrape of a shovel, and then, on closer examination, spied Billy mucking out the stall next to his filly, Storm. I'd forgotten how appealing Storm was: dappled gray with a white mane and tail. A horse like that would get me to Dog Hollow and back in style.

I cleared my throat.

Billy turned. "Why, hello, Fry. Delivery?"

Have I mentioned my full name? It's Georgina Louise Burkhardt. Now, Georgina doesn't suit me—it's the kind of name that has daisies growing out of it. But Georgie is fine by me and fine by everyone else too. Except Billy, that is. Billy McCabe has to have his own nickname for Agatha's little sister, and preferably something that points up his superiority in all matters of everything. It's not even enough to call me Small Fry. No, Billy McCabe has got to diminish the diminutive to Fry.

"No delivery. I need the loan of a horse," I said.

Billy laughed. "In case you hadn't heard, my family *sells* horses."

"Which means you've got a horse to spare! What about Storm? I'd return her in two weeks' time."

Billy leaned against the stall and smiled wide. "I've never even seen you ride a horse. As far as I can tell, you don't *like* the animal. A fine horse like Storm is more than you could handle."

Then Billy got serious. "Out with it, Fry. Where you think you're going?"

"I'd rather not say. What about another horse? We're practically family."

"Well, I'd rather not say whether or not I can help."

"One way or another, I need a horse."

"Tell me," he said.

"Dog Hollow," I said.

Those two words sucked the air right out of those stables. Billy groaned. "She's dead, Fry."

"Fine. I'm taking a look," I said.

"You took a look. You *saw* her body," he said.

"I saw parts of *a* body. Are you saying you won't help Agatha's little sister? That's cruelty, Billy," I said.

His eyes burned. "Pa was convinced—"

"Your pa was not convinced!" The words jumped out of my mouth, surprising even me. "Your pa hauled that body all the way from Podunk, Wisconsin, so Ma could identify it. He needed Ma to see it. If he were sure, he would have buried that body in Dog Hollow and brought back the dress. His word and that blue-green dress would have satisfied Ma. But your pa wasn't sure."

Billy crossed his arms. "Why hasn't she written? Thought of that?"

"Maybe there's a reason she can't write."

"That's a big maybe, Fry. Agatha would write."

I stamped my foot. "I am not here to discuss a dead body or my sister. I am here for a horse. I'd like to *rent* one, but if you insist—ignoring a close, near-blood relationship—I will *purchase* an animal. Which do you prefer?" I said. I took out my cinch sack and jingled it.

Billy's hand went up. "No. This is a fool's notion. I refuse to be party to it."

He put a finger in the collar of his shirt to get some air and glanced at the sky. "There's a storm coming. You should get home." He picked up the shovel and started to work.

I walked over and grasped his shovel. "Tell me what you and Agatha planned that day you kissed. You walked off whistling. I saw it."

I noticed how my words affected Billy. He paled.

"You saw?" he said, finally.

"You want to tell me what happened?"

Apparently, he did not. Billy did not say a thing. From the shelter of the stables I saw a fortress of cloud. A storm *was* coming.

I exhaled loudly. "What does it matter? You keep your

secret. But let me describe my particular state: I saw the two of you kiss. I told Mr. Olmstead. Mr. Olmstead threw over Agatha. *Then* Agatha ran off. There's a direct correlation between my telling and Agatha's leaving. If my sister is dead, I bear responsibility. If you think I'm going to accept a piecemeal body as evidence of my sister's death, you do not know me at all. Now, I've got money for a horse."

Billy's mouth moved like some semblance of language might escape his lips, but nothing came of it.

I leaned in. "I am not *not* going. I'll walk to Dog Hollow if I have to," I said.

"You shouldn't have seen that kiss," he mumbled.

I jingled the cinch sack. "Two dollars for the rent of a horse."

"Fry, there is no such thing as a horse rental."

"I'll give you five dollars. But I want a saddle, reins, saddlebags . . . all the horse-riding amenities," I said.

"Five dollars for a horse?" he said.

"You sold a pony to Pete Tarley for that."

Billy shook his head at me. "That's not the same. . . ."

"Why not? I'm thirteen. Pete Tarley's eleven and he acts like he's nine. Now, you don't have use for five dollars? I'm not asking for *your* horse. I'm asking to be treated like a customer with dollars in her pocket."

Billy blew air out his teeth.

"Ten dollars, then," I said.

"You don't have that kind of money," he said.

So I made a big show of opening up the cinch sack and snapped down five gold one-dollar coins on the top of the stall.

"Those are your Bechtler dollars," he said.

"That's right. Gold has more value than paper, and a *Bechtler* gold coin is the most valuable of them all. With the currency crisis, these coins are surely worth *twenty* dollars by now, but I'm willing to call them *ten*," I said. Gold having more value than paper and the Bechtler being the best quality gold coin were both things I'd heard Grandfather Bolte say more than once. But as to the actual worth of my coins? I had no idea.

Let me speak plainly, though: those coins were priceless to me. Not only were they every bit of money I'd saved since I was three, but Grandfather Bolte had told me that Bechtler dollars were minted with gold found by true prospectors. I liked to pretend they had Colorado gold in them since that was where Pa had gone to prospect. When Grandfather Bolte came across Bechtlers, he saved them for me, and I traded pennies, nickels, and dimes for those gold dollar coins. Still, my sister alive meant more to me than any coin.

Billy lifted his hat and wiped a line of dirt across his forehead. "Born stubborn and stuck obstinate," he said.

Hallelujah. His jab was a sure sign of his relenting. It was time to close the deal.

"Saddle, bit, reins too," I said.

He picked at the ground with the toe of his boot.

I went on: "You'll deliver my horse to Mount Zion Cemetery two days from now, on Saturday night, right before midnight. That'll give me a day to gather provisions. And you'd better not tell. Part of what I pay you for is privacy."

Billy raised his eyebrows. "It should cost extra for delivery at that time of night."

I picked up the five gold dollar coins from the top of the stall, counting them as I dropped them back into the cinch sack. Then I took his hand in mine, turned the palm face up, and placed the sack in it.

He met my eyes. Then he shook his head and closed his fingers around the sack.

Money was in hand.

The storm broke the moment my foot touched our front porch. Lightning ripped open that cloud's dark belly, and I watched the first drops hit the ground with puffs of dust.

It was the last rain until October.

CHAPTER FIVE

While I squirreled away provisions for my departure two days hence, I behaved in an unbearable manner. If caught in the same vicinity as Ma and Grandfather Bolte, I avoided their glances, wouldn't speak unless spoken to, and did my chores like someone who'd been shorted pay.

Ma's grief, in particular, wore on me like sandpaper. She dragged her sorrow room to room, and I found out that viciousness nested inside me. When I saw receipts left in the till, or noted that Ma had forgotten to mark down a sale, I mentioned it. I became a fault-finding expert: bins missing their lids, eggs gone bad, a customer left unattended, a boy in a fancy blue serge suit with a fist in the penny candy. I knew I shouldn't do it, but the part of me that was unredeemed spoke.

Ma gave me jobs like retrieving the canned delicacies from the cellar: fancy tins of tangerines, olives, smoked herring, Japanese green tea, lobster, and the like. I was to remove the dented ones (setting them aside for Ma to inspect) and polish up the rest. I was to do this on the back stoop—a place she wasn't likely to be.

Fine, I thought. *I can do without you too.*

I might be nasty as a snake, but I would observe decorum.

On Saturday night, I slipped between the sheets, curled into a ball, and, once again, feigned sleep.

As usual, I heard a fist rap quietly, and then the door haltingly creaked open. I heard the hush, hush, hush of dress fabric and the knock of shoes on floorboards. The bed sagged as Ma sat.

Callused fingertips pushed hair from my forehead.

"You're tired," Ma murmured. "So am I." I felt a puff of breath on my face, and then she kissed me good night.

How she persisted in her kindness when I could not stand the sight of her I do not know. I felt a flash of shame, not only because of my behavior over the past few days, but because beginning tomorrow morning, she would not find me.

Ma pushed herself off the bed as if she lacked strength. Her dress hushed. The door clicked close. I heard her footsteps grow quieter as she walked down the hallway. It was that sound, the sound of her footsteps, that echoed in my thoughts long after she'd shut the door to her room.

★ ★ ★

By eleven o'clock, I'd finished dressing and had written my note. I reread it:

> Dear Ma and Grandfather Bolte,
>   I need to see about Agatha. I will come home as soon as I can. I expect to be gone a week. I am sorry for leaving you, but had I told you my plans, you would have stopped me. Urgency impels me.
>
>   I love you,
>   Georgie
>
> PS I have taken some items from the store costing $2.23. I am good for it. I will pay all that I owe ~~upon my return.~~ shortly after returning.

I put that note in the center of the desk.

Then I went to get the Springfield. I'd had some luck with the rifle—Grandfather Bolte had cleaned it. He'd spent hours working on the barrel so that it would shoot straight. He usually did this kind of maintenance once a year, sometime in the winter. But since the funeral, Grandfather Bolte had busied himself with all sorts of odd jobs: oiling hinges, tightening the screws on shelf brackets, soaping the big plate glass window out front, and, evidently, cleaning the guns. On Friday, Grandfather Bolte handed me the newly cleaned Springfield. "That's a good rifle. You, Georgie, have got the touch for it. You're as good a shot as I've ever seen."

41

Even though I'd been angry at him, pleasure swelled inside me.

He gave my arm a little squeeze. "We'll have to go hunting soon. Would you like that?"

"Yes," I said. I smiled for the first time in days.

"Good girl. Bring it up to the gun rack, won't you?" he said.

I thought of this luck as I tied a rope around the Springfield and lowered it out the bedroom window. After it landed, I followed by climbing down the tree. I got the knapsack I'd stashed under some bushes and walked up the hill to Mount Zion Cemetery. At the cemetery, I sat with my back against the knapsack and waited for Billy and my paid-for horse with all the amenities.

An hour later, I heard horse hooves. I stood up. Billy was late, but all I could think was *My horse!* My heart pattered like it was Christmas.

I do not highly regard girls who get lathered up over horses: *Oooooh, cinnamon! I love a cinnamon-colored horse!* When an admired boy is riding atop an admired horse, it is a scene of such ridiculousness that it scarcely bears commenting upon. Yet here I was with sugarplum horses prancing in my head. I remembered a palomino mare (all gold and cream) in the McCabe pasture, and I somehow got the idea that Billy had tethered her behind Storm. This palomino was clip-clopping her way to her rightful owner—me.

Billy's cowboy hat appeared over the edge of the hill first. Then came his head, his shoulders. He was astride Storm. Even in the dark, you couldn't miss Storm—there wasn't another horse that set a hoof down with Storm's flair.

But where was my horse? My heart took a dip. I heard another horse, but I couldn't see it, and no one could hide a horse as large as that butter-colored palomino.

I leaned this way and that to see. When I couldn't, I ran around Billy's horse to get a decent look and saw . . . long ears. Extremely lengthy, awkward, and shaggy ears.

I watched the animal rest its blunt head on Storm's behind. Storm nipped at it, and in return, this animal brayed. "Bray" is much too short a word for the twelve-octave sound expelled from the creature's maw. It was part snort and part sneeze, all working up to a finale that can only be described as virtuoso-quality cow flatulence. I'd never heard such an utterance in all my life.

"What is that?" Those were the first words I said to Billy that night.

"A five-dollar horse," he said, smiling like he'd been looking forward to this moment for an eternity. "But I can't sell him to you. He's too valuable. So I'm loaning him. Isn't that what you wanted—the loan of a horse?"

"That," I said, pointing, "is not a horse."

"Why, yes, he is. Frederick here is half horse."

"And half donkey! I know what a *mule* is. A *mule* isn't what I *purchased*," I said. The darkness masked a lot of its mulish traits, but there is no getting around ample ears and the sturdiness of a mule's frame.

I eyed Billy atop Storm. In daylight, Storm looked fresh and crisp, as if she had stepped out of a mist that had left gray water marks on her white hide. I imagined riding this here beast of burden. My heart dove for my shoes.

Let me be clear: I do not like tricks or the people that play them. Ordinarily, I do not put up with it. But I knew Billy had me over a barrel. I needed to leave. And this mule— though with ears big as angel wings—came with tack, saddlebags, and even a holster for my rifle. It was transportation of a humble variety. If I could stomach the "humble," I'd be all set.

"You can go. You've done your bit," I said. I jerked my head in the direction of town.

"Don't you want your five dollars? I'm *loaning* Frederick," Billy said. That twinkle! Rude behavior through and through.

I put my hand out. "Better be my gold Bechtlers," I said.

Billy got down off Storm and rummaged in a saddlebag until he found my cinch sack.

He held it over my hand and gave me a meaningful look. "You put this in a *safe* place," he said.

I snapped my fingers and again opened my palm. Billy dropped the sack into my hand.

Yes, I made certain every one of those five Bechtlers lay snug inside.

"You sure are testy. I got you a ride and tack and you're not paying a cent. I'd say a 'Thank you, Billy' is called for."

I did feel a sting of contrition—infinitesimally small, but it existed. I could not deny that I now traveled with *more* money and on *free* transportation. My circumstances were improved. So I said it: "You did me a good turn. I appreciate it."

Billy nodded and we got to work.

Yes, we. Billy didn't leave right away. He seemed determined to help me load my supplies onto that mule, and I let him. I stuffed the knapsack into the bottom of a saddlebag, and slipped the Springfield into the holster. The holster was a perfect fit, which amazed me, given the length of the rifle. I knotted the sack holding my gold coins to a belt loop and tucked it inside my split skirt. And then we were done.

Billy walked over to Storm and mounted her. From the corner of my eye, I observed him, taking in all the details: reins in the hand that grabbed the saddle horn, one foot in the stirrup, and then hoist.

Doesn't that sound easy? It looked easy too. Except for the fact that I could not hold the saddle horn and skewer the stirrup with a foot at the same time. First, the foot. I swung my left leg at the stirrup—repeatedly. But the mule kept stepping, skipping, and, once, jumping as my foot neared its target. Finally, by holding the reins, I managed to keep that animal still enough to bull's-eye the stirrup.

Next? To get atop. Since a mile's distance lay between my hand and the saddle horn, I scaled that mule like he was the tree outside my bedroom window, handhold to handhold. I put one hand on a leather strap and grabbed a brass ring with the other. I heaved myself forward, aiming for the middle but ending with the saddle's stiff, upturned edge lodged in my gut. That brought water to my eyes, but I *was* on top. After some wiggling—and a few well-aimed kicks at stirrup holes—I found myself properly situated.

The mule did not appreciate my methodology. He skittered sideways, twisted his body around to see me, and finally brayed again.

That sound! A glance at Billy's back confirmed he had heard it. His shoulders pumped up and down in silent mirth. He turned Storm around to face me, but when he tried to speak, all he could do was thump his chest and laugh until tears rolled down his face. After a minute, he managed: "What are you *doing* to my mule?"

I would not grace that question with a reply. I kept up a solemn dignity, pretending there was no commotion beneath me. "You've done your bit. Thank you. Now go," I said.

Billy swallowed his amusement (which looked about the size of an orange). "You don't have to do this, Fry. You can sleep in a bed tonight," he said.

"Don't you worry about me. Good-bye. Off you go," I said.

The right side of Billy's mouth lifted slightly. "Alrighty," he said. He clicked his tongue, nudged Storm's sides with his heels, and started off. "Take care of yourself," he called over his shoulder.

I watched him go, giving a dry chuckle seeing his Spencer repeating rifle hanging in his holster. That kind of gun fit Billy to a T. Repeaters are the guns of amateurs—those who want the appearance of skill. A single-shot, like my Springfield, could be loaded quickly enough if a person practiced, but Billy McCabe couldn't be bothered with practicing. He had to have everything mechanized, and the Spencer held seven bullets in its buttstock, ready to fire. Of course, I'd shot a few repeaters now and again, but I preferred my single-shot.

Wait, I thought. *Why did Billy bring a rifle? Does he usually bring his rifle when he makes deliveries?*

I squinted and noticed a blanket rolled up behind Billy's saddle. And: *Are those saddlebags?*

Then Billy made a telling turn. He was not riding toward town, but heading to Miller Road.

Billy McCabe! I thought.

I prodded the mule's sides with my heels. Nothing happened. I pushed my heels into the mule's gut. Nothing.

"Come on, mule!" I said.

I nudged three times, hard. The mule tripped forward, snort-sneezed, and stopped.

"What is it? You're all conspiring against me? Move. Mosey. Get along." I leaned over and whispered into one of its ample, three-foot-long ears: "If you don't start walking, I swear I'll cut you into steaks and serve you for supper."

The ear pivoted and hit me in the nose. It felt like

velvet—finest quality velvet. Astonished, I touched it. The ear twitched away.

"What if I cook you with onions? Does that make a difference?" I said.

It did not. The mule refused to budge.

I exhaled, slumped in the saddle, and watched Billy, Storm, and that bedroll disappear from sight.

Then, without warning, the mule took off at a brisk trot.

I held on to the saddle horn for dear life. My knees bounced off the mule's hide like a wooden Dancin' Dan doll. That mule didn't slow until we were directly behind Billy and Storm.

I took advantage of the proximity to yell: "You're not invited."

"Oh, I'm going," he yelled back. I heard the little smile playing on his lips.

"Let me be clear: I am not the least bit fond of you. You do not want me as a companion."

"You want to walk?"

"That's immoral! We had an agreement," I said.

"That's right. And I did you one *better*—I *loaned* you that mule. If you take my mule, you get my company. Go right ahead and complain." Billy gestured at an upcoming field.

I gasped for retorts that would send Billy flying back home. I hate to report that not one came to mind. Instead, the mule slowed and I found myself wordless and gazing at a horizon filled with Billy's broad back.

This was a back arranged for veneration. Billy's shoulder blades jostled under a cotton shirt at least one size too small, highlighting his muscles. Furthermore, the hair on his head curled in a way that can only be described as in need of a trim and prideful. And the hat? That hat was called the Texas Cowboy High Crown and was made of nutria-belly fur, which was cheap, cheap, cheap. I knew because we sold that hat at the store. And Billy was no cowboy—the McCabes only owned one cow.

Evidently, this impostor thought he was coming along with me.

Unfortunately, I was tired enough to find a bed of nails cozy. I needed sleep. I decided to let Billy fantasize for now. In the morning, I'd set him straight.

We went about a mile, and then Billy pulled Storm up short.

"We'll stay here tonight. Start early," Billy said, assuming all authority.

I squinted and saw the outlines of a half-dozen shelters, a makeshift table, and some sort of fire pit. I slid off the mule. I undid my bedroll, grabbed the Springfield, and headed for the largest lean-to. I fell asleep as soon as I stretched my legs between the blankets.

I did not expect Billy to edge in beside me that night. Don't get the idea I offered an invitation. There were plenty of lean-tos to choose from, and Billy McCabe came into mine.

In addition to his largish frame, he brought two saddles, two bits, two bridles, and the saddlebags with him.

He made no effort to maintain quiet and peace either. The saddles thumped to the ground, the bits and bridles hit the earth with a jingle, and to make sure I'd awoken, Billy nudged my shoulder with a mud-caked boot. "Move over."

"Brute," I mumbled.

"Whiner," said Billy.

I kept my eyes shut, trying to make like I was half asleep, but I could tell he thought I was so, so amusing (once again). Made me want to lock my teeth on an ankle, but I have manners, so that sort of behavior would never do. I moaned appropriately, which caused Billy to let loose more chuckling, and then, yes, I scooted over.

I did peek. Consider it scientific (albeit anatomical) interest when I tell you that I watched as Billy stripped down to a worn union suit several sizes too small. I had seen boys' bodies at swimming holes, but never this close and never a manboy of nineteen years. (I would *not* call Billy McCabe a man.)

The one verifiable *man* I had seen in a union suit—Grandfather Bolte—had a body like steel on hinges: strong, functional, but rather mechanical. I don't mean any disrespect, but my grandfather's body was about as interesting as a printing press, a butter churn, or a clothes-washing wringer. And while machinery might incite curiosity, it rarely fascinates.

But Billy? Through the threadbare cloth of that union suit, I read Billy's movements in a cursive of muscles and tendons that contracted and stretched across his back. You could not read my sister's body like that, nor mine—our muscles weren't so well elucidated. Moreover, Grandfather Bolte's body steamed through the world, bending habitually on worn creases. But with Billy's body I got the sense that anything could happen—he could twist, leap, spin every which way without thought. When Billy put his foot right near my face (of course) to shove a saddle into place, I watched the muscles above his ankle undulate like underwater plants. Billy's body was *all* ease.

As much as the body before me was a revelation, I noticed something mundane too: the patch job on that union suit. The stitches were neat—many times tidier than mine. Who'd done that stitching?

It came to me: Billy had done it. Whereas my family overflowed with women, Billy's family was devoid of them. As the oldest, Billy had taken on many tasks himself, including patching and sewing. I'd watched him mop a brother's chin more than once.

I'd heard Billy tell the story of the birth of the youngest McCabe boy. Billy had been eight years old. He'd sat on the front porch waiting while his ma travailed. He heard every bit of his ma's labor because it was a hot summer night and the windows of the house were thrown open to keep his parents' bedroom as cool as possible.

Finally, his ma's cries went quiet. He heard a whack. A tiny voice pierced the night. The sound brought Billy to his feet in pure wonder. He heard his pa's quick footsteps coming down the stairs. The front door opened. Billy turned grinning.

But when his pa appeared on the porch, he was not smiling. In fact, his pa saw Billy only to hand him a tiny wrapped infant (his fourth brother). Then his pa ran back inside, taking the stairs two at a time. Twenty minutes later, the midwife came out. She gathered the boys together for what she called "sorrowful news."

Billy said then that he did not need to listen to the midwife's words. He'd heard his pa crying. When the infant in his arms joined in the crying, Billy went into the kitchen to warm some milk.

In the lean-to, Billy sprawled out with his head on a saddle and fell asleep. He took up most of the available shelter. He smelled of horse. I suppose I smelled of mule. But horse smells worse. After all, a mule is only *half* horse. Even so, when Billy shifted and his back touched mine, I let it rest there.

Before you think anything, know that it was a cool night and Billy exuded heat. But it was a mistake to let his back touch mine, because without warning, I felt a howling ache. Agatha and I often slept back to back.

I could not sleep now. That's when I noticed a strong smell of rotting pigeon in the air. I thought of what I knew of pigeons and remembered a particular day in February.

CHAPTER SIX

Trying to guess the plans of wild pigeons is folly. The direction they go is their own business. Likewise, it's near impossible to know where they'll roost for the night, let alone build a nesting. Their movements defy theorizing and deducing (though fools persist). Pigeons come and go as they please.

The way they'll come upon you will catch you unawares too: Sometimes the pigeons are like a towering thunderhead in front of you in all boldness and in numbers too great to count. Sometimes they're as inconsequential as a litter of leaves rolling in the distance, and they pass in and out of the periphery of your vision without notice.

But whatever the configuration of pigeons that confronts

you, when they leave, they are *gone*. Those birds move *together*—as if they have one mind and one set of wings.

In 1871, I experienced wild pigeons on three distinct occasions. The first time was in February, when I saw a small, easily frightened group. I spotted them once. Then they were gone. In March, I saw pigeons a second time. This time they were the mighty cloud that Agatha spun underneath. These pigeons also left. And then there was the third time: in April, the pigeons returned and nested in our woods, not five miles west of Placid, Wisconsin.

The first time I saw the pigeons—the twenty-eighth of February—was a day coming after a long freeze and little sunlight. Day after day had glowed dimly, and night had slammed down at four o'clock in the afternoon. Because of the cold, my fingers refused to do small work and I marched around the store to get blood into my toes. I had thought I would like being free from school. (I'd finished my sixth year of winter school the year before.) But no schoolwork only made the dark hours endless.

That particular morning I awoke and saw the sky—a blue-sky day! By midmorning, everything outside glinted with running water. It ran along the edges of snowbanks and trickled down icicles. Drips hitting pans pinged in the store. By afternoon, patches of earth—red, brown, tan—appeared on the sides of hills. Everybody in the world came into town that day, with weeks of stored-up talk. They told jokes, described how they planned to lay out their crops, and whispered that they'd near gone mad during the long, dark days. Then they finally got to business and bought the supplies that had supposedly brought them into town.

Agatha and I were about as helpful as two squirrels. We skittered through the store, trying to stay near the plate glass window. We offered assistance carrying packages (I swear, some the size of postage) out to our neighbors' wagons to feel the sun on our skin and smell the air. Finally, Ma had enough of us, and said we should go ahead and run it off. "Don't make me track you down for dinner," she said.

We didn't wait to be told twice. We raced to get our coats. Agatha put her sketchbook and pencil in a satchel, and I went up the stairs to grab the Springfield from the gun rack in the hallway.

Of course, Agatha gave me *that* look when she saw the rifle.

I tried to change the topic by pointing at the sketchbook bulging in the satchel. "What are you going to sketch? It's winter," I said.

She touched the Springfield. "You always end up killing something. I don't know how you can be so sure about putting creatures to death."

Months later I would ruminate upon this remark: *I don't know how you can be so sure* . . . But at the time, I lumped it together with her other overly sensitive statements. I'd seen Agatha kill spiders. She seemed *sure* enough then.

Agatha glanced around and said what we both knew to be true: "We need to leave before Ma changes her mind."

We pushed out the door and ran down Main Street. It made an abrupt turn over the railroad tracks and went right by the train station before lining up with the Wisconsin River.

As usual, Agatha decided our direction, but I thought she went toward the river for me. She knew I liked looking at rivers anytime—winter, summer, spring, whenever. And that day, near the rapids, spray froze to tree limbs and hung sharp from ledges. I put the Springfield down, found some rocks sprouting five-foot icicles, and knocked the ice free. "On guard!" I yelled, holding an icicle like a sword. Agatha picked up another, and we fought, sword-fight-like, until there was nothing left but stubs. Somehow, we both ended up stuck in the same snowbank and cackling hard.

After we'd extricated ourselves, I picked up the Springfield and we started to walk again, talking the whole way about everything and nothing. We sang as many verses as we could remember of "My Darling Clementine" and made up several more. We discussed how much ginger was required to make a good ginger beer and argued about whether a diamond-shaped kite or a box kite was better for flying in the fierce wind at Mount Zion Cemetery. We made plans to start a moth collection, find a bear's den (I promised not to shoot), track down some honeycomb, and climb up to Flat Rock, where we'd spend the night watching for comets.

Then Agatha turned at a split-rail fence, and I realized she was heading toward the McCabes'. Or, to be more accurate, toward Billy McCabe.

Had she wanted to see Billy this entire time? I'd wanted to be with *her,* and here she was thinking about Billy?

Billy McCabe had corrupted my sister's character. It began the moment he and Agatha became best friends at that town picnic on the bluff. Billy was fifteen, Agatha was fourteen, and I was nine. The two of them went off to explore a cavern with "an echo like a cathedral." (Some words a person remembers with exactitude.) I followed, keeping up until Billy ruffled my hair with his pawlike hand. "Why don't you play with Ebenezer? He's your *age,*" he said.

I rolled my eyes at Agatha, sure she'd agree that Billy McCabe's pea-brained presence was no longer required. We, the sisters, would go off on our own. We'd leave the dimwit behind.

Instead, Agatha shrugged. "You don't like caves, Georgie. Stay here. You'll have more fun."

Oh yes, that stung!

Agatha and Billy had been friends ever since. From then on, everybody in Placid assumed that Billy and Agatha would tie the knot.

This blue-sky February day was only two months after the New Year's ball. Ever since that ball, the situation had felt tentative. I'd been watching Agatha closely, sure all it took for disaster to strike was Agatha showing weakness where Billy was concerned.

If spending your blue-sky day on someone wasn't a

consent, then I didn't know what it was. Meet Mrs. Billy McCabe! Billy would take Agatha off to some barely settled, territory-like place in Minnesota and I'd never see her again. Apparently, this was all fine by Agatha.

I stopped right there. "I'm not going that way," I said.

"What?" said Agatha.

"You're asking me to spend time with babies so you can be with Billy."

"Georgie, you *like* those boys fine."

"The McCabe boys think the most ignorant things are funny. All they'll want to do is shoot this rifle."

"That's what you want to do."

"Not like that, I don't." I kept walking down the road.

Agatha stood at the turnoff watching me. "Where are you going?"

I turned around to face her and said loudly: "To be by myself. I don't *fancy* the McCabes like you do: Billy, Billy, Billy."

Her face screwed tight when I sang out his name like that. "Suit yourself. Be back here in an hour," she said.

I walked on without saying anything. Our first free day, all that bright blue sky and melting snow, and Agatha wasted it. She'd do worse too: she'd ruin everything. She'd leave our family. She'd leave *me.* In an hour I expected to see Agatha and Billy perched on the McCabe fence, holding hands, ready to share their "announcement."

Let her. I do not need her, I thought.

I more or less clomped down the road, losing all sense of blue sky. When I reached a field, I turned into it and headed toward the woods on the other side.

I was three-quarters across when I saw something rooting around on a patch of snowless ground underneath some black oaks. It stopped me short. I looked twice to be sure. But that rosy chest was unmistakable, and those birds are not exactly small—wild pigeons.

February 28 was mighty early. People talked about pigeons sending scouts, but I'd never believed them. Scouting suggested intelligence, which everybody knew pigeons lacked. But there they were: about twenty-five of them feeding on acorns at the field's edge. They called to one another, each note higher than the last: *kee-kee-kee-kee*.

Back came my blue-sky day. It had alighted on earth in the slate-blue feathers of the male pigeons' backs. The rose color on the males' chests eased into the blue by turning green and gold. Long black tail feathers trailed behind.

I couldn't believe my luck. I put the rifle in my left hand and rooted around in my coat pocket for a cartridge. Then I opened the trapdoor, slid the cartridge in, and closed it back up.

Most people shoot pigeons with a shotgun—No. 8 pellets. A single cartridge of pigeon shot is filled with hundreds of tiny balls. These pellets spray outward, so a single shot can garner several birds. But I wasn't after a pigeon pie; I wanted sport, to show skill at shooting. Grandfather Bolte and I were keeping track of what I shot with the ammunition I used, and to shoot a bird with a single bullet is difficult—even a bird as large as the big male in front of me. I estimated that bird at a full seventeen inches head to tail. *He'll do fine,* I thought.

The movement had captured the big male's attention. He twisted his head this way and that, eyeing me. Several other birds flicked their heads side to side, and began to take a few tentative steps. I heard a low *twee* repeated among them. The wing feathers on one lifted a little. I think of wild pigeons as being bold, but I could see this group would bolt if I did anything sudden.

This is the moment where inexperienced hunters panic. They sense anxiety in their prey and jerk their rifle to get their shot. But I never panic. I let stillness seep through me while I line up my target.

Given my preoccupation with Agatha and Billy, achieving stillness that day was no small feat. But I did it. I leveled the rifle and concentrated on that big male. That bird and I existed in a tension, like a wire was pulled tight between us. I could hear him thinking: *What? What? What?* The big male twitched his head to look at me from one more angle. Then that male took a step toward me, his rosy red breast dead center. I squeezed the trigger.

Bang! The rifle butt jammed against my shoulder. A bird screeched. Wings clapped. A trail of smoke hung in the air.

I let the barrel drop. As I waited for the air to clear, I shook out the cartridge and loaded another one into the rifle. Maybe the birds hadn't flown too far.

When the smoke cleared, the big male lay on the ground right where I expected him. The rest? Gone.

I walked over, picked the big male up, and ran my hands over his feathers. I flushed with pleasure imagining what Grandfather Bolte would say. I removed the unused cartridge from the rifle, pocketed it, and remembered Agatha and Billy.

Agatha was sitting on that split-rail fence alone.

"Where's Billy?" I called out.

"I nearly went looking for you, but I didn't know which way to go," she said.

She hopped off the fence, came to me, and began to fuss. "You are covered in mud. Your shoes are barely recogniz-able," she said. Agatha pushed me in a circle and tugged on my skirt. "Ma is going to have words with you!" Then she clutched my hand and held it up. "For heaven's sake, hold that bird out from your coat. The blood, Georgie!"

I saw that the wool of my coat was soaking up the bird's blood, red blossoming on the dark gray.

"What were you thinking? This is going to take a week of cleaning." Then she looked at the bird. "What a beautiful pigeon!"

"February is early too. Where *is* Billy?" I said.

But Agatha wasn't listening. She was pulling me toward a puddle. "We need to clean that coat before you go home," she said.

So we splashed water all over me and my clothing, trying to remove the grime. My skin came clean, but any cloth with pigeon blood on it was a lost cause. Agatha kept fretting over the stains.

Finally, I shoved Agatha off me. "Did you tell Billy you'd marry him or not? I asked you about Billy twice," I said.

That stopped her. Agatha stood up, shook off her wet hands, and put her mittens on one at a time. "You are so ungrateful. Here I am helping you and you act like this. Shame on you."

"Did he ask you? What happened?" I said.

"What business is that of yours?" she said.

"If you leave, it's my business," I said.

She huffed, then flicked up her hands. "No. I'm not marrying him. I told him no. Feel better?"

"He asked you today?"

"No, I gave my *answer* today. Now stop meddling. You get so doggedly determined. Sometimes I'm not surprised that things end up dead around you."

A mean-spirited remark was what I called that. I took off at a good clip.

Agatha ran in front of me and put out her arms to halt my progress. I stopped when I saw the tears on her cheeks.

"I'm sorry, Georgie. We've got the store, right? There's always that."

"You and me?" I said quickly.

"You and me," she repeated. I did notice she stated it with little excitement. But the fact she said it at all made me happy.

The male pigeon made Grandfather Bolte happy.

I *was* in trouble, though. I do not recommend icy puddle water for cleaning up on blue-sky February days. When we got home, Ma took one look at me, grabbed the pigeon from my right hand, and told me to get out of those clothes. She wrapped me in two wool blankets and set me in a chair by the kitchen fire. Even with the heat of the fire, my teeth chattered.

Still, a blue tinge never stopped anyone from being in trouble. Ma turned my coat over in her hands. "How could you be so careless?" she said. I saw Agatha smirk.

Grandfather Bolte saved me by walking into the room and seeing that bird. He held it like I'd brought back a brick of gold.

"I swear," he said. He ran his hands over the long tail feathers and started asking me questions: Where had I shot this pigeon? How many did I see? He wanted to hear every last detail. He listened closely.

Then he gave me a wide smile. "One shot?"

I nodded.

He put his hand on my head. "Figures it was you that got this bird."

Ma glanced between the two of us. "You spoil that child," she said to Grandfather Bolte.

Grandfather Bolte smiled at me again, and began to pace. He grabbed a packing slip, turned it over, and scribbled. Then he threw down the pencil and continued his pacing.

He paused briefly in front of me. "Anybody see you bring this bird here?"

"I don't think so," I said.

He clapped his hands. "Good . . . good."

The next thing I knew, Grandfather Bolte had his coat on.

"Where are you going?" said Ma.

"Cooper for barrels," said Grandfather Bolte.

"Can't that wait until after dinner?"

"Let me be, Dora," he said. He jammed on his hat, and slammed the door behind him.

Ma looked startled. Agatha and I glanced at each other, smiles creeping onto our faces. We always thought it was funny when Ma became Grandfather Bolte's little girl. Ma spotted our grins, and pointed a finger at me. "Don't think I'm done with you."

First, Ma made me pluck that pigeon. Second, I was to clean my coat. (I would wear it until worn, no matter the stain.) Third, I was given two weeks of extra chores.

As it turned out, I wasn't the only one in trouble. Grandfather Bolte ordered so many barrels that it caused consternation. At one point, I heard Ma say "gamble" and "risking everything" before I was found too close to the door and sent back to work.

But that wasn't the last of Grandfather Bolte's spending. I found that packing receipt he'd been scribbling on. It was a list of things pigeoners bought. It was a *costly* list too, like he *knew* those birds would nest in our woods. Ma was right on that score: buying all that was gambling, and worse than card gambling. A person may become skilled at predicting cards, but not at foretelling nestings. There is no sure way to anticipate a pigeon's preferences in terms of place. Soon as you do, they'll nest two hundred miles away. Any pigeoner worth his salt will tell you the same.

Of course, when it all worked out, and Grandfather Bolte made all that money, he was hailed as a business genius. No one called him a gambler. Not one.

CHAPTER SEVEN

Lean-tos are the most paltry of shelters. I do not recommend them. Still, I have to admit that the first night of my journey—despite Billy, despite the memories of pigeons and Agatha—I slept.

I awoke, however, to a spider diving, arms wide, for my chin. The spider stopped short and hung—its knot of eyes staring. I blinked and it pivoted, pulling itself back up into the twigs of the lean-to. If that wasn't unpleasant enough, I turned over and rolled face-first into the spider's previous knitting. As I frantically wiped at my cheek, something popped several times in succession under my elbow, followed by a disagreeable wetness. I jerked upright into a seated position, and put my head into more spiderweb. When I was finally able to check my sleeve, I saw two caterpillars (or what *was* two caterpillars) soaking into the plaid.

There's a reason I appreciate civilization.

Worse, it stunk. I had smelled the air the night before, but it wasn't until the morning that the smell of rotting pigeon threatened asphyxiation. *Better get used to it,* I thought. To-day the road I'd follow—Miller Road—would pass straight through what was left of the pigeon nesting. If these were the foresmellings, I expected nothing less than fully ripe putres-cence by, say, ten o'clock.

Then I heard the sizzle of bacon in a pan. *I'd* brought bacon. *Billy!* I twisted around and saw Billy's neatly folded bedroll. I reached for the nearest saddlebag, and found none of my food. Then I remembered my food was in *another* saddlebag. Billy had helped himself!

And why not? He apparently did whatever he pleased.

Billy was a situation in need of resolution.

I ran through my morning ablutions: wiped the sleep out of my eyes, rebraided my hair, and pressed my clothing flat with my hands. I found the cinch sack with my five Bechtler dollars. It would never do to suspend my gold dollars that way. So I sat down, pulled off the split skirt, and stitched those gold coins into the waistband. Finished, I patted it. *Fine.*

Now, Billy McCabe. I dug through the saddlebag again, and pulled out *The Prairie Traveler.* I opened it to the table of con-tents, expecting something like "Getting Rid of Unwelcome Guests." What did I find? Not a word! I had to make do with skimming any topic remotely associated with unwelcome situations: storms, stampedes, rattlesnake bites, grizzly bears, and the ways of the "western Indians." (Captain Marcy's description of those western tribes did nothing less than scare me half to death.) In general, this "handbook" contained not one hint about solving relational difficulties. Reading it, you'd think that once you'd chosen your company of men, everything would go on all buttercups and roses until the day—*alas!*—you parted. Captain Marcy was most unhelpful.

I'd have to put my foot down and tell Billy—in no uncertain terms—to pack up and go home.

Would that work? I doubted it. But if it didn't, I'd leave him in the night. I was not traveling with Billy McCabe.

A thought jolted me: Ma and Grandfather Bolte would find my note *soon*. They'd send out the troops, especially after losing Agatha. *Move!* I thought.

I crawled out of the lean-to and stood up.

I was not expecting what I saw: the world was *feathered*.

Feathers were everywhere. Tiny barely there feathers floated in the air, while larger feathers carpeted the ground. The barely there feathers caught on bark, limbs, and leaves; others clumped together and rolled in dirty balls. Several were tangled in my braids. I examined one and saw that the feather was pale blue, the same color as the morning light. Under my feet, flight feathers—brown, gray, and black—covered the ground.

It came to me where we were: we had slept in a deserted pigeoner camp. The flight feathers on the ground were clipped (the ends of wings, half a set of tail feathers). I saw a stained makeshift table with hay all around. And I located the feathers, piled as high as me at one end of the clearing. The wind had pushed the heavier flight feathers aside, leaving the under-feathers free to snag the air. From where I stood, it looked as though the pile smoked tiny pale blue feathers.

I wondered why no one had collected those feathers for feather beds, quilts, and pillows. Pigeons are hunted for meat first and foremost. But usually the feathers are *utilized*.

What if these feathers *had* been utilized? What if every person who worked at this camp had taken what he could use or sell?

This had to be the camp of one of the wild-game dealers. Those people traveled the rails to find wild game to sell to big-city markets, then hired local people to do the work. Only an operation of that size could produce this kind of surplus.

How many pigeons had they killed? A lot.

Yes, there had been a lot of pigeoners in Placid, I remembered.

You'll recall my sister spinning underneath the pigeons: Remember how Agatha beckoned me to come? Remember how I was overwhelmed by fear and did not step off that porch? That was the second visit of pigeons, in March. They left after that second visit too, and no one knew if they'd be back.

After the second visit, Placid was filled with waiting and

watching. The pigeons had yet to choose a place to nest, and we desperately wanted them to do so in our woods. We followed news of pigeons in the newspapers, asked the station-master repeatedly what he'd heard. Some rubbed their lucky rabbit foot. Others offered up plea-filled prayers. If those pigeons came back, we'd all be rich. A nesting meant weeks and weeks of barrels of pigeons to sell, *and* the accompanying influx of pigeoners. We in Placid would be ready to supply anything those pigeon hunters might need or want. And after the eggs hatched? There would be the babies, the acorn-fattened squabs—a delicacy for discerning big-city palates, and a moneymaker for our Placid, Wisconsin, pockets.

It was during this waiting period in the beginning of April that Grandfather Bolte went hunting with Mr. Benjamin Olmstead. As Mr. Olmstead scared up a covey of bobs, he mentioned my sister. My grandfather was so taken aback at the mention of Agatha that he jerked. He tried to shoulder his gun, but the stock ended stuck in his armpit. He didn't bother pulling the trigger. Mr. Olmstead, however, fired into the clapping, and three bobwhites tumbled from the sky.

My grandfather asked him to repeat what he had said. As Grandfather Bolte remembered it, Mr. Olmstead then said: "I'd like to court your granddaughter Agatha—with your permission, of course." Grandfather Bolte said the richest man in our county had difficulty meeting his eyes.

I suppose it was a few days later—right after dinner—

when a knock came at the front door. Grandfather Bolte answered it. From the seclusion of the kitchen, the rest of us heard Mr. Olmstead's voice. He asked if he could go for a walk with Agatha.

Ma, Agatha, and I looked at each other, confused.

Agatha got up, started to undo her apron, touched her hair, and then glanced at Ma. Ma was beside her in an instant, helping.

"You don't have to go. He's only rich," I exclaimed.

Ma gave me a hard look. "Wait for me here. Don't leave that spot until I come for you."

Then Ma put a hand on Agatha's back. "Let's get you changed." They both went upstairs.

A minute later they returned, and while I seethed in the kitchen, I heard the usual sorts of greetings between Mr. Olmstead and Agatha. It was the kind of thing you might read in *Godey's Lady's Book:* "I wondered if you'd go for a stroll with me, Miss Burkhardt." "It would be my pleasure."

It was like that. I do not mind telling you that I did not care for hearing that sort of language in my own home. I nearly laughed out loud when Grandfather Bolte called the night "fine." It certainly was not! April rain had mucked up the road, and there was enough bite in the air to make your nose run. But out went Agatha and Mr. Olmstead into that "fine" evening.

I never doubted the evening's outcome, though. Poor Mr. Olmstead! Agatha would refuse his courtship because Agatha would never get married. She'd said as much that February blue-sky day. What was marriage when you could live life encumbrance-free by running a store with your sister?

But I did not foresee that Agatha would come back from that walk carrying a book. It was a hefty tome entitled *Ornithological Biography,* written by a man named John James Audubon. Apparently, there was an entire library of these sorts of books, all about flora and fauna, at the Olmstead Hotel.

That night, up in our room, the book was laid open on the desk. I peered at the page before I got under the rugs on our bed: "Passenger Pigeon, *Columba migratoria.*" I read on silently: "The Passenger Pigeon, or, as it is usually named in America, the Wild Pigeon, moves with extreme rapidity. . . ."

I turned on her. "You *can't* see him. You asked me to run the store with you, remember? We made a pact."

Agatha laughed. "We did not make a pact."

"You did! You asked me to run the store with you."

Agatha frowned. "Did I?"

I huffed. "In February? The day I shot the pigeon? You said, 'We've always got the store.' You said you and I would run it. You did."

Agatha tilted her head as if she were trying to dislodge the memory. Then she remembered. "I was upset, Georgie. That was the day I turned Billy down."

"You *said.*"

"When you're eighteen, you'll understand. . . ."

"What does age have to do with keeping your word?" I said.

"What has got into you?"

"Are you going to see Mr. Olmstead again?" I looked her square in the eye.

"I don't know," she said.

Later, I saw the way she ran her hand along the spine of that book.

Then—lo and behold—the wild pigeons came back to Placid. We could not believe our good fortune. Everyone, including the newspapers, had said they were gone from our area. Even Grandfather Bolte had grown despondent. Yet here they were—back again in April. A miracle! It was the third (and final) visit of pigeons in 1871. But this time they were here to *stay*.

The pigeons hovered over the woods in a thunderhead for two days, April 17 and 18. Then the thunderhead settled on the forest and it became a nesting. The newspapers called it the largest pigeon nesting "within recorded memory." This nesting was shaped like a capital L lying on its side. The short end went up north fifty-five miles. The long end went west seventy miles. Altogether the nesting covered one hundred twenty-five miles. In addition, the thickness of this letter L nesting was between six and ten miles. It was a *big* nesting, and Placid, Wisconsin, was only five miles away.

Word of the nesting traveled from one rail station to the next, newspaper to newspaper. Men, women, and children came by train, steamboat, and wagon, on horseback, or by foot. The trains from Milwaukee, Chicago, and St. Paul doubled and tripled their runs to accommodate the extra passengers wanting to go to Placid, Wisconsin. Pigeoners (some professional game dealers, most opportunists) came from every corner of the United States—Pennsylvania, Michigan, Illinois, Massachusetts, Alabama, and Louisiana (to name a few). Several clans from the Winnebago and Ojibwa set up camp along the Wisconsin River. The countryside was covered with tents, lean-tos, and open-air sleepers. All these people gathered around the nesting in the woods. Suffice it to say, I'd never seen so many people. I could barely cross the street without a struggle!

The atmosphere reminded me of a holiday gone on too long. Gin shacks sprung up along the river overnight. When the birds flew overhead (which they did somewhere between two to four times every single day), gunshots flared from porches, a cellar door, and even from the outhouse behind the blacksmith's. One drunkard danced in the pigeon sleet, fired into the winged mass, and caught the falling birds in his cap. Bands of children abandoned their chores and wandered the hills with sticks and boards to hit the birds out of the sky for the pure fun of it.

I watched Mrs. Hazeltine come out with a frying pan! Her belly, six months pregnant, preceded her. She stepped off her porch and stuck that fry pan into the flight path. The pigeons came so fast and hard—whack, whack, whack—they pushed Mrs. Hazeltine backward across the street as if she were a sailboat with a fry pan for a sail and pigeons for wind.

I took part in it too. I could not resist shooting the Springfield out our bedroom window. The sky was so thick with birds that a single bullet brought five or six tumbling from the sky. I retrieved them from our garden like late-autumn squash.

Most nights Agatha and I fell asleep to the sound of drunken singing on Main Street. A few times it was accompanied by a guitar. (I do like guitar.) Sometimes Grandfather Bolte slept in the rocker on the front porch with the double-barrel across his lap to, as he put it, "help prevent foolishness." This boiled down to making sure no one shot rifles too near our property, or tried to rob our store.

No one went hungry and that's a blessing to everybody. I am sure every table in our corner of Wisconsin held a pigeon pie (pigeons cooked in a broth, walnut catsup added, covered with a crust, and then baked twenty minutes). In addition, all those who kept their minds on working could make some money.

The Bolte General Store was a hullabaloo every minute the doors remained unlocked. If there was a hint of a sale to be made, Grandfather Bolte made sure it transpired. PIGEON-ING SUPPLIES! WE SELL *EVERYTHING* A PIGEONER COULD WANT

OR NEED! read one sign in our front window. Ma, Grandfather Bolte, and Agatha advised, recommended, gathered, and packaged. I restocked and kept everything clean. Cleaning meant never-ending scrubbing. Outside, I scrubbed pigeon lime off porch floorboards from the birds' twice-daily flights. Inside, I cleaned up after the pigeoners: tobacco spit, and nesting whatsits tromped in by their boots.

Unbelievably—in the midst of all of this—Ma and Grandfather Bolte allowed Agatha to leave anytime she wanted as long as it had something to do with Mr. Olmstead. So while I scrubbed floorboards (wearing away precious knee skin), Agatha went off on a "walk."

Mr. Olmstead and Agatha even visited the pigeon nesting. Trudging through pigeon lime, enduring a stench of epic proportions, and using burlap sacks as hats to avoid getting covered with pigeon excrement should have sunk their courtship, but Mr. Olmstead and Agatha had such a good time they went back a few days later. When they went a third and fourth time? I started thinking that Mr. Olmstead must truly care for my sister. Why else would a man let himself be shat upon by thousands of birds?

Did Agatha return those affections? I didn't know. To be truthful, I was beginning to attribute evil to my sister's motives. See, Mr. Olmstead gave Agatha full access to the library at the hotel. During the time they courted, Agatha could be seen walking to and from the Olmstead Hotel with a book under one arm. The study of birds—ornithology—was the topic. At the end of the day, I'd fall into bed exhausted while Agatha sat at our desk reading.

I told Ma and Grandfather Bolte my suspicions straight out. I walked up to the two of them and said: "Agatha is keeping company with Mr. Olmstead for his books. That's a sin. You need to put a stop to it."

Grandfather Bolte took the pipe out of his mouth and laughed. Laughed! "You worried about your sister's eternal damnation? You leave that between your sister and God. Who do you think collected those books? It's called having similar tastes."

Ma put her hand on my head. "It's a good match, Georgie. Leave it be."

Those books made me feel my first bit of sympathy for Billy McCabe, though. Billy had known Agatha for years and years and he had *never* given her a book—not once. I saw how lending Agatha those books was like dangling a worm before a sunfish. Agatha couldn't help but bite.

Of course, by then it was generally known that Billy was courting Polly Barfod. I heard people talk about the situation, and the consensus seemed to go something like this: Though it was doubtful someone of Mr. Olmstead's station would choose Agatha, *if* Mr. Olmstead chose Agatha, it was for the best. Agatha's beauty would surely go to seed after a year or two of homesteading through Minnesota winters. Better for Billy to choose a Dane like Polly—someone with cold winters in her blood, and the strength to stump a field.

★ ★ ★

It was the beginning of May when I saw Agatha and Billy kiss. I knew then that Agatha did not love Mr. Olmstead, because Billy walked away with a whoop and a whistle. My sister loved Billy *and* Mr. Olmstead's library full of books.

It's funny how months of memories can flash through a person's head in moments. How many minutes has it taken me to tell you? Five minutes? Ten? But for me, I stood upright in that pigeoner camp and did all of that remembering in under a minute.

Billy called out: "You going to stand there all morning? I've got bacon."

I looked over. Billy squatted by the fire, shaking a skillet over the flames. As I'd suspected, *my* saddlebag sat open next to him. The audacity! That was *my* bacon.

And then I thought of Polly, Billy's fiancée. What was Polly going to make of Billy and me traveling together? Everybody knew that Billy had loved Agatha. Now, despite his promises to Polly, Billy had run off with Agatha's little sister. To make matters worse, we were heading to the place where Agatha's body was supposedly found. Billy being here was unmistakable evidence of a divided heart. If I were Polly, I would break my engagement and not look back. The question was this: Why was Billy risking *everything* to be with me? This was more than a simple favor. This trip *meant* something to him.

I watched Billy pull another slice of *my* bacon out of the waxed paper in which I had carefully wrapped it. He waved the bacon at me and flipped it into the pan.

Did this have something to do with that kiss? Maybe something had been planned. Was Billy meeting Agatha? But wouldn't that mean my sister had staged her own death?

No. Not possible. I could not believe it.

"You wouldn't dawdle if you knew how good this egg biscuit is."

It would not do to send Billy away, or to sneak off in the night. Billy McCabe was part of this puzzle. I needed to keep an eye on him so I could figure out what was going on.

"I am not your manservant, Fry. Come here. Eat," said Billy.

I laughed at that. "Don't get feisty. I want to leave as much as you."

I walked over and took the plate out of his hand. Seeing that plate of bacon, eggs, and biscuit made me groan. The biscuit was perfection: browned golden on the top *and* bottom. Grandfather Bolte says I make a masterful blackened biscuit. I took a bite, and gasped at the pure delicacy of Billy's biscuit out in the wild.

"Good, huh?" said Billy.

"It'll do," I said. No boy should be able to cook like that. It isn't natural.

We sat there eating for a moment and then he said: "Aren't you going to tell me to go home?"

"You can come," I said.

"Why? I was sure you'd want to fight about it."

I chuckled, delighted that this time Billy was amusing me and not the other way around. "Why not? I can use a good hand. You did a nice job with our mounts last night. You've proven your worth." I reached up and grabbed a tiny light blue feather out of the air. Without warning, Agatha's story came to mind. *Feather by feather she picked out her path.*

Billy stared at me, huffed, and then got up. "I am not your 'hand.' You clean that plate and I'll teach you how to saddle."

I tell you, I enjoyed that exchange greatly.

CHAPTER EIGHT

Dadgum mule.

I nudged that mule with both heels. I nudged him hard. Nothing. I jerked my body forward in the saddle, hoping the movement would communicate what I wanted. Yes, that mule's right ear swung some in my direction, but otherwise he was chewing. I could see this mule demanded nothing less than my entire dignity.

Meanwhile, Storm, bearing Billy up in style, clip-clopped, clip-clopped out toward Miller Road.

It was time to go. That note lay right on top of my desk. One of my chores was to start the stove, so as soon as Ma and Grandfather Bolte walked into a cold kitchen, they'd seek me out.

It wouldn't be difficult to track me either. In the same way Agatha's path was no secret, neither was mine. Agatha had traveled with the pigeoners on Miller Road toward Prairie du Chien. Where was I going? Like always, where Agatha had gone.

I did not know if I'd go all the way to Prairie du Chien, though. My plan was to start by finding out what I could in the town of Dog Hollow. I also wanted to look around the spot where the body in the blue-green dress had been found. With those two things done, I'd know better what came next.

That long-ears was still chewing. We had moved, but only to a preferable patch of grass.

"Stubborn, no-good, bat-eared mule," I said. I poked him repeatedly with my heels and then gave up the fight.

My eyes watered because of the stench from the nesting. I twisted around, pulled out a colored handkerchief, and secured it over my nose and mouth.

Billy would have to return for me. He'd see me marooned on the back of this mule and take his amusement. Then a tether would be rigged up, attaching the long-ears to Storm. Yes, I'd be traveling to Dog Hollow like a load on the back of a pack animal.

So be it, I told myself. I'd suffer a hundred such humiliations if it brought my sister home. At least there wasn't one more surprise Billy could spring. After forcing both this mule and his company on me, what else could he do?

At that moment, the long-ears jolted into life. He lurched forward into his pounding trot. I cried out, clamped my knees against the saddle, and lunged for the saddle horn, breathing a sigh of relief when I grasped it solidly between my hands. The reins slipped away, gone—lollygagging beyond my reach under the mule's neck. Meanwhile, my rear end clapped loudly against the saddle leather, every muscle declaring its complaint.

Then we were right behind Billy and Storm. Billy swayed left, right, left, right with Storm's gentle gait.

Does this sound at all familiar? Because I recalled something similar occurring the night before.

Billy didn't even turn around. *As if* he didn't hear us.

But this time the long-ears—*my* mount—stuck his muzzle in Storm's tail. I've never been so embarrassed for an animal in all my life.

Storm bared her shockingly big yellow teeth. The long-ears stumbled backward and I held on.

Now Billy turned, laughing. "You should see the look on your face."

"This mule is *in love*! You chose this mule *particularly*," I said.

Billy leaned for my reins, which dangled under the mule's jaw. "Try these. You might find them useful." He handed them to me.

Never underestimate Billy McCabe's ability to produce the unpleasant surprise.

Then he clucked his tongue. Off he and Storm went. Where Storm went, the mule went. Since I was riding that mule, I went too.

The Prairie Traveler fails to mention that sitting on a mule, following two wagon-wheel ruts from point A to point B, is not stimulating activity, particularly when your traveling companion does not talk and everything passes by at mule speed (clip, pause, clop, pause).

We did cross paths with several groups of people on Miller Road. The first was a family in a wagon. As soon as I saw them coming toward us, I started to root around for the photograph of Agatha. Then it struck me that sixteen days had passed since Agatha had been on Miller Road. This family was most likely passing through. My questions would have to wait until Dog Hollow. When other groups of people passed us, I nodded a greeting and did not say more.

Meanwhile, we entered the pigeon nesting. We came upon it in the deepest part of the forest, where the trees grew tall and thick, and we stayed in it for ten miles. It looked for all the world like some sort of deserted battlefield. Twig nests were ripped apart, and what was left hung in streamers from the branches, or lay clumped on the ground, which was a stew of pigeon dung, nesting material, and rotting pigeon (heads, feathers, and guts). Flies loitered, and a sucking sound accompanied each hoof step.

I averted my eyes by looking up, and that was where I saw unsullied nests. Way up high, the nests cradled between limb and trunk and then lined up one after the other on the strong, straight branches. I started counting the nests by twos (two, four, six, eight . . .). Twos were too slow, so I counted by threes (three, six, nine, twelve . . .). I got to fifty-one and then ninety-nine nests—all in one tree.

I wondered what Agatha had made of this.

The mule did not care for the nesting. He grew twitchier and twitchier, his ears shifting back and forth. Any rustle made him hop. (Yes, mules hop. I can testify to it.)

I tried kindness. I stroked him and patted his side, telling him that what had happened on this land had happened long before we got there. I pleaded. I coaxed. I whined. I even sang him little mule songs made up on the spot.

His antics had started to make me nervous. "You're giving me the jimjams, Long Ears," I told him.

But Long Ears paid me no mind. He was mesmerized—mesmerized, I tell you—by scraps of sound. Far ahead of us, Storm strolled along, flicking her tail like she didn't have a care in the world. I noted that the distance between us and Billy and Storm had lengthened substantially. Next thing I knew, they were completely out of sight.

A mile or two later, I saw a swath of sunshine ahead on Miller Road. "Look, a clearing. That'll be nice. You'll feel better, right?" I said.

But this wasn't the woodland meadow I imagined. Instead, felled trees lay in spiky piles, left where they'd been chopped down. About thirty vultures perched, their fleshy heads picking at something they'd found in abundance. I drew my breath sharply when it finally occurred to me that these trees had been chopped down to get at the squabs, the baby pigeons.

It was in that pile of trees that Long Ears began to shimmy from side to side.

Then Long Ears stopped outright. He craned his neck.

I saw it—a badger. It gulped something down, and slipped between two logs. Seeing one creature, I saw them everywhere: crows, raptors, skunks, and another badger. This forest crawled with carnivores. I pressed my heels gently into Long Ears' side. "Keep moving. We'll be fine," I said quietly. I leaned over and patted him.

But Long Ears became unbearable. I couldn't keep him moving forward. He tried to turn around. He walked sideways (something I thought only trained circus horses did).

I rooted around in my saddlebags until I found the sugar, and pinched a stuck-together chunk. I put it under his lips.

Long Ears would not touch that sugar.

I sat up. "I am doing my best. What is wrong?"

That was when Long Ears turned one hundred eighty degrees. He backed up and brayed.

I thought the two of us were finally communicating.

We were not.

Right there and then, a cougar leapt out of the woods.

CHAPTER NINE

I froze. My body did, anyway.

My mind, on the other hand, jumped over the moon and ran off with the spoon. It listed what it saw by every possible name. It thought the list forward: *Catamount, cougar, American lion, painter, red tiger.* It thought it backward: *Red tiger, painter, American lion, cougar, catamount.* My mind pinched the list in the middle, folded it over, and thought it again: *Painter, cougar, catamount, red tiger, American lion.*

It distressed me to discover that running vocabulary lists was my mind's behavior during direst need.

In addition, no one *sees* these cats. As far as I knew, they kept to themselves. I was quite sure that Grandfather Bolte and Agatha had never seen one, because they would have *talked* about it for weeks.

I had seen a skin once—claws attached, mouth propped open showing teeth as long as my pinkie. But let me explain: a floppy fur does not compare with what blocked the road, tail twitching.

Long Ears had turned us around, so we were on Miller Road but facing the direction we had already come, toward Placid, Wisconsin. The cougar stood between us and Placid, square in the middle of the road. It was as tall as a butter churn. From head to hindquarters it looked about the length of our kitchen table. Both my arms put together didn't make the thickness of that tail.

I sat stiff as a twig on top of that mule and looked at *it*. It looked at *us*. The cougar didn't threaten. It seemed merely interested. But its demeanor didn't matter; I saw that cat and I *knew* things—for instance, where I lay in relation to the dinner plate. *Georgie hocks. Georgie hambone. Georgina sweetmeats. Smoked Burkhardt bacon. Ground Georgina Louise. A rump of Georgie to roast.*

Then something Grandfather Bolte once told me bellowed through my head: "By the time you see a catamount, that catamount has been following you for at least half an hour."

That cat had eyed my neck! It's a skinny little neck too.

Then the cat began to pace back and forth, its eyes on *me*.

Long Ears took a step backward. The movement jarred my body awake. "Whoa!" I grabbed the reins and pulled, meaning it for the first time in our acquaintance. Lo and behold, Long Ears stayed put.

Gun.

A thought—hallelujah! I'd begun to believe my mind's only talent was chitchat and parlor games.

I reached into the holster and pulled hard on the butt of the gun.

I pulled much too hard.

The gun came out of the holster quick, hopped on my hands (as I tried to grab it), and landed at the feet of the mule. It lay in muck two feet below my right foot. It might as well have been in San Francisco—I could not get off that mule to get it.

I looked at the cougar. The cougar hissed. Its ears went flat against its head. It took a step toward us. Then one more.

Help me, God. My heart scampered in my chest.

Long Ears started to rotate. He was thinking of turning our collective back on that cat. I *knew* that was a bad idea.

I pulled on the reins a second time, yanking his head around so that he faced the cat. I clamped my heels into his sides. Once again—I could barely believe it—Long Ears listened to me. He did as I asked.

But now that I was facing the cougar, what was I supposed to do?

The Prairie Traveler.

This was the thought that came. I know what you're thinking—I thought it too. It was hardly the time for flipping through an index! Is it under "catamount," "lion," or "painter"?

Still, my right hand reached into my saddlebag and grasped

The Prairie Traveler, all 340 pages with maps, illustrations, and thirty-four itineraries for the principal wagon routes between the Mississippi and the Pacific.

And then, seemingly without permission, my right hand threw it. *The Prairie Traveler* spread its cardboard wings, flapped once, and made a satisfying smack on the cougar's snout.

The cougar batted it away. The book twisted, hit a tree trunk, and plunked down in pigeon lime.

Now the cougar paced. Back and forth it went, hissing all the while.

Again I reached back. And again. And again.

Everything I touched I threw: my tin cup, my plate, the gray-striped blouse, a fork, my jacket, rope, a jar of jam, the sewing pouch, a bar of castile soap, the whetstone and belt knife. The soap and jam made contact with the cougar's hide. The plate skipped like a stone and veered east. I had some luck with the belt knife, though. I threw it like the lady knife thrower I'd seen at the circus. It struck the cat's paw. Unfortunately, that only made the cougar spit in a fearsome manner. It drew back its lips, revealing molars, incisors, and fangs, all of significant proportions.

I kept at it, though. As I threw, I yelled: "Get out of here, cat! You don't belong here, cat! Go home, lion! I've had it with you! Get! You evil, nasty thing! Get!"

I waved my arms, shook my fists. The movement heated me up. If that cougar had so much as touched me, I would have ripped it apart with my bare hands. And I'd have done

one better than Samson of the Bible. I would not leave a cavity large enough for bees making hives.

Long Ears jerked this way and that. But he obeyed me when I pulled him square. I made sure to keep our eyes fastened on those tawny ones.

Then my extra pair of bloomers flew from my hand. The bloomers punched out on a puff of wind, and I noted how each of Ma's hand-sewn pleats looked like a fold in a cloud.

What I am saying is that I looked *away* from the cougar.

Long Ears brayed.

I realized my error and twitched to look back, but the damage was done: the cougar had crouched. Everybody knows that isn't a good sign.

"Billy!" I yelled. (Don't know why I didn't think of that sooner, but I did not.)

As the cat shifted onto its left rear paw and then its right, time slowed to a dirge. Faces played like a magic lantern show: Ma, Grandfather Bolte, the sheriff, all the McCabe boys lined up tallest to smallest, and, of course, Agatha, Agatha, Agatha.

The cougar and I eyed one another for a long moment. I gave that animal my meanest stare.

And then—I swear—that cat lay down. Right there in the middle of the road, it lay down like it might take a *nap*. Like a big old barn tomcat. A moment later it got up and walked off the road.

That made me mad. After all that—after it crouched

down and made my heart rattle against my ribs—the cougar walks? I found a spoon in a saddlebag and hurled it at that cat. I said things loudly that I do not care to repeat. Anyway, the cat was out of my throwing range. It bounded up the hill on my left, sprung over a log and around a rock, then strolled up the rest of the hill.

Billy arrived full gallop, gun across his lap.

He pulled Storm up, and followed my gaze. When he saw the cougar, he shouldered his gun and fired once, twice, three times. The cat mounted a rock, gave us a backward glance, and disappeared over the crest of the hill.

"It's out of range," I said, my mind displaying its genius once again, since this was obvious. I looked at him. "Particularly for a repeater."

Billy tugged at my holster. He looked around. "What happened to the Springfield?"

"I drew it too fast. Didn't load it either." My voice shook. My body followed suit.

Billy noticed, and laid a hand on my shoulder. "I'd like to see that thing dead," he said.

"I never thought I'd catch sight of one," I said.

Then Billy got down from his horse and picked something up. He wiped it off with a sleeve and walked over to me. He handed me *The Prairie Traveler.*

I took it. I felt so grateful for that book's fortitude that I welled up.

"You seem to have lost a few of your things," he said.

I looked around me. Everything I owned lay strewn about, most settled in pigeon muck. Half of it I did not remember throwing. My colored handkerchief lay in the middle of the road, emblazoned with hoof marks.

I got down off the mule. I picked my white bloomers from a wild rosebush and waved them like the flag of surrender. "Thought I was done for," I said.

I was trying for a joke. It did not work. I gasped, covered my face with one hand, and cried.

Billy put his arm around me, and I leaned into him.

CHAPTER TEN

The nesting ended in stutters—a walnut tree with twenty nests in it, a scrub oak with eight. The smell remained heavy as lead. But there came a moment when I removed my dirty, hoof-imprinted handkerchief. It was well into the afternoon by then, the light starting to soften.

Most of what I remember about that time is how I trembled after that cougar. I kept envisioning oversized barn cats amusing themselves with half-dead mice. Billy rode behind me—a necessity because the hairs on the back of my neck stood up like lightning rods. Snaps of sound made me jump.

Then the shadows lengthened another foot and we arrived at a secluded cove along the Wisconsin River. I looked at Billy and he nodded.

I pulled Long Ears to a halt, got myself disengaged from the saddle by yanking on my left knee (my stiff muscles produced a yowl that caused me to see red), and then proceeded to free Long Ears from tack of every configuration.

Billy rode Storm straight into the Wisconsin River. When I looked over at the two of them, I saw him cleaning pigeon lime from Storm's legs and from under her belly.

I appraised Long Ears. He was in worse shape. My mule was shorter than Storm, and therefore had been closer to the pigeon ordure. That run-in with the cougar probably hadn't helped either. Still, this mule had done his part. More than that, he'd tried to warn me when danger lurked. Now he stood patiently, waiting for me to finish my task, despite the slowness with which I did it. I smiled at him and ran my hand down his side and then his muzzle. This mule might have had an unfortunate face, but otherwise he possessed a cornucopia of admirable characteristics. I decided then that I did not care to ride any other animal. Long Ears had done me a good turn.

"Sweet, sweet mule," I whispered into one of his absurdly large but velvet-soft ears.

Then I led him down to the river to clean up.

Billy came over with a hatful of water and drizzled it over Long Ears' back. Long Ears grunted and lifted his muzzle toward Billy.

"On your head, is that it?" Billy cooed as he poured the water down the mule's face. I swear Billy came close to kissing that mule.

That was enough for me. (If you must know, I felt a touch of jealousy.) "If you're going to care for Long Ears, I'm taking a bath," I said loudly. Perhaps I said it a little too loudly. After that cougar, the only thing I wanted was to scrub that day off my body.

Billy looked at me with eyes gone soft with pity. I saw he understood I'd been badly scared.

I couldn't have that, so I gave him my sternest stare. "I'd like to see these animals hobbled and a cooking fire started by the time I'm through bathing. Then I'll make dinner for the two of us. Think you can manage that? Or is that too much responsibility for Billy McCabe?"

That wiped all the pity out of his eyes. Billy pretended to be startled, stood up straight, and then made a deep, deep bow.

"What does that mean?" I said, making sure to spice up my tone with some whiplash.

"Not one thing," said Billy. But as I walked away, Billy whistled "God Save the Queen."

As soon as I was out of Billy's sight, I knew I'd made a mistake by leaving him. The shakes came back strong. A blade of grass would shift and I'd notice. Every odd breath of wind made me flinch. I nearly yelled when leaves brushed up against one another.

But cougar or no cougar, I craved a bath. I tucked myself behind a grassy bend in the river where I could see a scrap of

Billy. (I hoped he could not see me.) I tore off my garments, and scrubbed my body and clothes hard.

After I'd scoured myself raw, I wrung out the clothes and pulled them on wet (I would not wear undergarments in front of Billy), and hurriedly washed everything I'd tossed at the cougar. I laid these out flat on bushes to dry. Finally—hallelujah—I was done. I stumbled back to Billy as fast as my sore muscles would take me.

When Billy asked if he could take a bath before dinner, I said "Fine with me" as casually as I could, but it was all I could do to not run after him.

"Cat got your tongue?" said Billy. At his words, heat rose up my neck and bloomed in my face. I'd twitched my way through his half-hour bath, feeling stalked at every moment. Now that he was back, I did not want him out of my sight.

Then Billy stretched out his long legs and pushed up the brim of his hat with the back of his hand, and I saw it. I finally perceived what every girl saw when she glanced at Billy McCabe: the square chin, the eyes that became half-moons when he smiled, the muscles in legs long as the horizon. Billy McCabe was well made. It was like looking at woodwork done by a true craftsman. And truth be told? I *enjoyed* gazing upon him.

Now, do not get any ideas. I *knew* Billy McCabe. I knew every one of his opinions, presumptions, and annoying traits. How I *wished* Billy McCabe was only a block of carved wood!

Billy squinted at me, concern written across his face. "I'm sorry, Fry. I should not have said 'cat.' I don't know what I was thinking."

I'd forgotten that he'd said "cat got your tongue." I nodded. (Nodding being about all I seemed to be able to do.)

I studied my dinner plate. It startled me. I'd concocted a meal of noteworthiness. I'd fried up the last of the bacon, broken it up into bits, poured in canned beans, and tossed in my version of biscuits (store-bought) so they'd soften. The label read MADE TO TRAVEL. I was sure those biscuits would soften in the beans and be suffused with the savoriness of bacon—as delicious as Billy's homemade biscuits had been that morning.

I looked over at Billy and felt something cozy.

I had to admit the feeling felt *overly* cozy.

Gratitude—that's all it is, I told myself. It was to be expected after the day's events.

Billy put one of those biscuits between his teeth and bit down. It worked like a doorstop; his mouth stood ajar. He removed the biscuit with two fingers and placed it on his tin plate. The biscuit pinged.

But what *had* Billy done to make me feel so grateful? He hadn't scared away the cougar. I'd done that myself.

Still, I could not seem to talk to Billy. My tongue would not work.

Good gravy, I needed to clear my head. The best way to do such a thing was to come directly to the point. So I cleared my throat (to make sure I was capable of language) and then said: "Polly will not be happy when she finds out you're traveling with me. So what is it, Billy? Why are you risking your engagement? I'm guessing you still love my sister. Tell the truth. I'm done with wondering."

Say something like that and you expect a reaction.

I did not get it.

Frankly, Billy seemed unperturbed. He held the biscuit to a back molar, tried gnawing it, and then set the biscuit on the plate. Again, it pinged. "These biscuits are harder than diamonds."

"Guaranteed to keep six months," I said.

"We are not going to California—only to Dog Hollow, and that isn't even to the Mississippi."

I took up a forkful of beans and bacon, chewed, and swallowed. "But why are you here? When Polly gets the news, she'll break off your engagement," I said.

Billy observed me for a moment and then spoke. "*Loved*. I *loved* Agatha. It's past tense, Fry."

Then he picked up the skillet and dragged that diamond-hard biscuit along the scummy edge. "Do you remember that day in February when the two of you came up to our place? I didn't see you but Agatha said you went hunting? You remember?"

I exhaled audibly. Billy was going to take his own sweet time getting to the point.

"That was the day she turned me down," he said, responding as if I'd nodded.

Billy shook something off his fingertips, put his plate on

the ground, and settled back against the log. "I'd asked her to marry me before that. By then, I had asked her so many times I lost count. Think I started when I was fifteen. She laughed—always. But in February I got down on my knee. I said, 'I mean it, Agatha. I need to know.' She said, 'I can't.' I said, 'Can't or won't?' She didn't answer right away. Finally, she said, 'Won't.'"

I stared at Billy more than I listened to him. Why wouldn't he simply tell me why he'd come on this journey? It seemed like there was something he wasn't saying.

Again I wondered if Billy was meeting Agatha out here, somewhere. But that seemed far-fetched. I could not believe Agatha capable of such willful deceit. To make her family believe she was dead? No—it was not within the bounds of possibility. I'd have to imagine Agatha wrapping a body in a blue-green ball gown. The Agatha I knew could not shoot a sparrow.

No, she would not be able to hurt her family, let alone treat a body with such disrespect. Whatever Billy was hiding, it was not a meeting with Agatha. It was something else.

As Billy continued his reminiscing, I began counting days, working out the time line of events. I started with the kiss—a fist in the air, a whoop, a whistle. I saw the kiss on a Thursday, the first week of May. I went to see Mr. Olmstead the next day, on Friday.

The worst part (and the part I never wanted to admit)

was that a moment before I spoke to Mr. Olmstead, I knew I shouldn't say a word. But up until that moment, I possessed absolute certainty of the rightness of my cause. I would have said, with confidence, that my sister was seeing Mr. Olmstead for his library. (Beware of such convictions, for they are fraught with peril.)

See, I'd never seen a room like Mr. Olmstead's study. Books were everywhere. Books lined the walls. Books were splayed open on the seats of chairs and were piled in corners in precarious-looking stacks. (And *why* were there so many books in his study? Agatha had told me there was a hotel *library*—there wasn't enough room in his *library* for these books?) What wasn't filled with books was taken up by collections. Butterflies, from white to purple, had been lined up, pinned to a board, and framed. Another frame held hundreds of beetles in shades of blue, green, and gold. An osprey, wings spread, stood guard in one corner, a badger in another—both stuffed, of course.

But the most startling item was a book open on a pedestal. This volume was abnormally large. Each page was two feet by four feet, and the book was laid open to an illustration of two birds. Those birds breathed on the page. The female (in yellows, olives, and browns) perched on a branch above the male (in blues, black, salmon red, and white). The female leaned to place something in the male's beak. The male stretched his beak upward to accept, arching his neck. I traced their necks with a finger—yellow feathers to olive feathers to a red, upturned throat. A bit of text from the opposite page caught my eye. It read: "I cannot describe to you the extreme beauty of their aerial evolutions."

I knew those birds. They were wild pigeons. "Extreme beauty" written of pigeons? But who would even take the time to see the beauty of pigeons—let alone paint them? And then to print an enormous book with two pages devoted to the birds? It was an insanity. Pigeons were not important birds like, say, eagles. And pigeons lacked intelligence; they were not noteworthy in any manner, except in their abundance.

Of course, I knew who would describe the beauty of pigeons: my sister.

Also, the author of this big book.

And, after seeing this study, Mr. Olmstead.

"Isn't it something?"

I jumped. But of course Mr. Olmstead had been sitting behind his desk the entire time. He had watched me take it all in.

"My steward said the matter was of utmost importance?" He smiled. Why hadn't I noticed his blue eyes before?

I shook my head, confused by what I'd seen in this room and unsure of my purpose. I stepped toward the door.

Mr. Olmstead laughed. "I shouldn't have frightened you. Please, Georgie, tell me. Whatever it is. Particularly since you came all this way." He gestured at a chair. "Please."

My hand stuck to the doorknob. I couldn't sit. I couldn't go.

What Grandfather Bolte and Ma had said was true—Agatha and Mr. Olmstead seemed to be made for one another.

But I *had* seen that kiss.

I told him in a blurt.

Mr. Olmstead winced. He rapped his fist on the desk. "Did you know we are engaged?"

"No."

Mr. Olmstead read the disappointment on my face. "I'm sure they meant to tell you. It was only three days ago. Your store has been busy. We did want to keep it quiet, though, because every one of my relations will descend on this town when they hear the news. I'd like to give Placid time to clean up after the nesting."

Ma *had* tried to tell me something. We *had* kept getting interrupted.

He looked at me. "Did you ask Agatha about the kiss?" he said.

"No," I said.

I heard his fist rap the desk again.

"Thank you for telling me," he said. He got up, walked around his desk, and opened the door. His face had gone still. I could not read it.

"I'm sorry," I said.

He nodded.

I left.

By Monday, I was fairly certain that Agatha had been thrown over by Mr. Olmstead, because she stopped talking to me. On Tuesday, I overheard my sister explaining to Ma that Mr. Olmstead did not trust her and that she could not marry a jealous man.

Agatha gave me the silent treatment for a week. The next Monday night, May 15, the nesting broke and Agatha told me the story of the old man and the white pigeon. Ten days after that, she ran off with the pigeoners. That was Thursday, May 25. Now it was sixteen days since she'd run off, and here I was a runaway too. I'd run off with Billy McCabe in order to search for her.

I looked across the fire at Billy—the whistler, the whooper, the kisser. If anyone knew what that kiss meant, it was Billy McCabe. But when I'd asked him about it on the day I negotiated for a horse, all he'd ended up saying was that I "shouldn't have seen that kiss."

Anyway, what did it matter what the kiss meant? If I hadn't told Mr. Olmstead, my sister would still be in Placid, her funeral would not have been held, and I would not be out here searching for her.

I glanced again at Billy and willed myself to stop ruminating. I was like some old cow on her cud, continually re-chewing wilted, partially digested conversations. Find Agatha. Go forward. That should be my plan now.

Billy folded his arms across his chest. He'd been rambling on and on about Agatha, oblivious to the fact that my mind had been elsewhere. (Some people *assume* your attention. It *is* annoying.)

Billy continued: "I needed time. I could have convinced her if it weren't for Mr. Olmstead. He turned her head, gave her ideas. Agatha was mine." He huffed. "It was underhanded and rude of the man to court her like that. Mr. Olmstead owns the entire world and he had to have the one thing that mattered most to me."

Mine? Thing? I would give my right foot if Agatha thought she was *owned* by Billy like some *item* stocked on a store shelf. "I don't remember any rule that says someone is *yours*. Agatha didn't even say she'd marry you. She didn't *have* to marry you. On that February day, Agatha asked me to run the store with her. She wouldn't have married you—no matter the circumstances."

Billy sniggered. "That was your plan, huh?"

I didn't like that "heh heh" at all. "You must have believed her. You started seeing Polly."

"I thought it would bring Agatha around," he said.

My jaw dropped.

He pointed a stick at me. "You can't say a word of that. I love Polly. I do. I don't want to discuss this. You're too young to understand," he said.

"I'm only too young when it suits you," I said.

"It is *not* your concern," he said.

I glared at him and got up to clean my plate in the creek.

We sat silent awhile, each of us engaged in our own tasks. I finally joined him by the fire in order to clean my rifle. The

Springfield was covered with pigeon muck, and I needed to know that it would fire without a problem. I promised myself I would be ready next time, shooting dead any cougar contemplating a meal of girl and mule. As I worked, honey light soaked into a deepening blue sky. Moonlight spattered the water, and clouds of tiny white insects floated up from the banks.

To test my cleaning job, I loaded a cartridge into the Springfield and aimed at a twig approximately one hundred yards away. I fired. The twig shattered.

"Nice shot," said Billy.

"I never miss," I said.

"I have heard that when you're *holding* the rifle, you're quite good."

He'd caught me off guard and I laughed. "I do need to work on my draw."

Billy grinned. "Let's not fight. I like you when we're not fighting."

It was a simple enough statement, but somehow that statement stopped my tongue in its tracks. "Yes" was all I managed to say in reply, though I suddenly wanted to tell him that he hadn't been as bad a companion as I'd imagined he would be.

Then Billy yawned. "That's it. I'm going to bed."

At that, my neck hairs lifted straight off my skin. I saw cougars stalking me, dragging me off, my screams muffled by the sound of river water passing.

I set the Springfield across my lap. "I'm going to sit up," I said.

Billy waved away fire smoke to look at me. "We've got a long day tomorrow."

"If you're tired, go to bed."

Billy laid his eyes on me. "Fry, that cougar isn't coming back. It went straight over the hill, remember? You scared the bejeebers out of it." He smiled. "Like I expect you would."

I shook my head. "No, Billy, listen to me. Today I learned I need to pay attention. Long Ears was the one that heard the cougar—not me. I'm keeping my eyes open," I said. I began to shake.

"It was probably only curious. You and Frederick are a pretty big target."

"Go to bed."

"I shouldn't have let you get so far behind."

"Even if I wanted to sleep, I couldn't. Go."

Billy frowned. After a moment, his eyes lit up. I watched as he pulled a canvas tent from his saddlebag and set it up. He opened my bedroll inside it and set a saddle at the top for a pillow. "How does this look?" he said.

He was right. I liked the idea of canvas walls all around me. He said he'd sleep in front of the tent with the repeater by his side.

Then Billy reached for my hand. As his hand wrapped around mine, a sort of wooziness came over me. I stood, but I swear my feet were not on solid ground.

This confused me, but I *had* confronted a cougar. Ever since that cougar, my senses seemed off, misfiring every which way.

Billy walked me to the tent, lifted the flap, and let go of my hand. "It'll be fine. I won't let anything get you," he said.

As I went to sleep, I may have thought of Billy, but I dreamt of Agatha. I dreamt of that night—years and years ago—that I woke up and found Agatha gone from our bed. I crept through the house and finally found her in the vegetable garden out back, the wind twisting her nightgown around her ankles. Barefoot, I ran into the garden to meet her. The two of us, in white nightgowns, stood hand in hand between rows of carrots and lettuce as we watched comet after comet scuff the sky. I felt garden dirt between my toes, and liked the way her hand fit around mine.

But in the dream, her hand slipped from my own. It was like she wasn't even trying to hold on.

CHAPTER ELEVEN

After more lessons in mule saddling, Billy and I rode all the next morning. We arrived in Dog Hollow as the sun beat down overhead.

I'd heard Dog Hollow described as down-and-out, distressed, and in straitened circumstances, but nothing could be further from the truth. Not one thing sagged, leaned, or needed oiling, and there were plenty of inhabitants. The railroad had come through Dog Hollow about five years previous, and people say rail transforms a town. Consider Dog Hollow transformed. Dog Hollow was a full-fledged community as big as Placid. The Smoke River—a tributary of the Wisconsin—ran straight through its center.

As we crossed an ample wooden bridge, I noted the

town's amenities. I saw two inns—the American House and the Ellwood House. We passed a flour mill, a foundry, a sawmill, and a brewery. This was beyond the usual townlike accoutrements—the blacksmith, the general store, the churches (Methodist and Lutheran), and the harness shop. The water-powered sawmill did look aged, but it had been painted a bold red, and from within its walls came the ear-piercing buzz of board-making productivity. Pigeon lime streaked several porches, but that was the same everywhere.

We tied up at a watering trough in front of the Dog Hollow General Store. Long Ears and Storm plunged their snouts into the trough and began to drink.

"Don't mind if you do," I mumbled, feeling that some sort of etiquette had been breached when they started drinking before I'd dismounted.

Billy gave me twenty cents for some bread and hard cheese from the store, mentioning the inedibility of my biscuits. He said he planned to see about repairing a buckle on one of his saddlebags, and then to stop at the butcher. He had a taste for sausage roasted over a fire.

A cowbell clanked when I opened the door to the general store. The sound reminded me of home. But all similarity to our store stopped with the cowbell.

Two women took up space on the floorboards—one behind the counter and one in front. The woman behind the counter frowned, looking at me with pin eyes in a face that was as hard and as expressionless as a plank. She was the width of a door frame, she'd yanked her salt-and-pepper hair into a bun, and she wore a red blouse with girlish ruffles. She leaned on that counter like she hadn't the strength to stand upright.

The second woman, spectacled and wasp-waisted, turned to take a lengthy look at me.

"I'd like a loaf of bread and some hard cheese, please," I said. I used my best Sunday-school articulation.

With good customer service you expect a little hup-hup, one, two, three. Old Pin Eyes, though? She didn't even straighten up out of her lean. In fact, she leaned farther forward, and her rather significant ruffled chest nudged a jar of butterscotch candies to a precarious position at the counter's precipice. "Let me see your money," she said. She held out a hand.

Asking for money first? I sent her a flinty look in reply.

"I don't know you from a darn hole in the wall," she said.

That burned me up. I could feel those five gold dollar coins stitched into the waist of my skirt. I sure would have liked to show her a couple. I settled on dangling my two dimes in front of her face.

She made to take one.

I jerked both hands back. "I need to *see* your cheese and bread first," I said.

"I'll come by tomorrow," said the spectacled woman to the woman behind the counter. As she left, she cinched up her purse and her face at the same time. She made sure I saw it too.

The unpleasantness went on like that. There were heaves and sighs, eyes rolling like marbles, and much trundling back and forth. Pin Eyes brought out farm cheese and two-day-old bread. I took it anyway, along with two licorice sticks for me and a box of sugar cubes for Long Ears. (I planned on working on the mule's affections.) At the end of our transaction, I had to *tell* Pin Eyes to wrap it up. When she asked for twenty cents, I pointed out I'd only bought *fifteen* cents' worth of goods. She replied that if I didn't care for the price, there was another store in Owatonia—only thirteen miles out of my way.

As I gathered my parcels in my arms, I paused to consider whether I should ask Pin Eyes about Agatha. Ask the rudest woman in Wisconsin? Why? I wanted to wash my hands of her.

But I knew I had to do it. If you only talk to nice people, you won't find out the half of it. Nice people either keep their noses so clean they hardly know a thing, or they conveniently forget what they know and fill their heads with daisies. You've got to talk to the rude ones as well.

"Excuse me. One more thing," I said.

The look on her face told me turning had taken significant effort.

I held out the framed photograph of Agatha. "I'm looking for a young woman. Her name is Agatha Burkhardt. She's eighteen. A little shorter than you. With auburn hair."

Pin Eyes took the photograph. She ran her finger around the edge of the frame.

I continued: "Agatha came through here two and a half weeks ago. She was traveling from Placid, Wisconsin, with three pigeoners—a married couple and a single man."

I paused, and then added: "Also, if you know anything about a body found on Miller Road about eight miles outside of Dog Hollow, I'd like to hear about it. The body was difficult to identify."

Pin Eyes handed the photograph back to me. "Who is this girl to you?"

I could see in her eyes that she would not talk unless I told the truth.

"My sister," I said. I did not want to say that. Every time I said "my sister" out loud, water gathered in my eyes. It happened then too. I could not control it.

Pin Eyes looked away (a kindness I noted). Then she spoke: "I hear things now and again. What I heard was that the Placid sheriff took that poor girl's body back with him, saying he thought he could identify her. Our sheriff said that given the rough condition of the body, it was difficult to say what happened."

Pin Eyes gazed out the plate glass window. In the light, her eyes were walnut brown. "I lost both my brothers in the war. A friend delivered a letter from Josiah, the youngest, telling us that if he died, we should know he'd made peace with his Lord and Savior. But Luke? We never found out what happened to Luke. I hope someone buried him. It is not right for someone to die in service to their country and have no one tell their family."

"You're *assuming* my sister died," I said.

She looked at me incredulously. "Has she written?"

I pressed my lips together.

She reached out and touched my elbow. "Maybe she'll write," she said.

I saw in her eyes she *meant* it.

"Thank you, ma'am." I blotted my eyes, gathered my purchases and the photograph, and quickly left.

I glanced back at her one last time and saw that plank-hard face again. I did feel bad, though, about calling her Pin Eyes, and I suddenly realized that her girlish ruffles made sense if you thought of her age at the time she lost her brothers. It seemed likely that after hearing about the death of *two* brothers, a person might lack the desire to consider clothing. In addition, I was beginning to understand how the past can seem more alive than the present. I thought of Agatha all the time.

Outside, I put the purchases in a saddlebag, reserving a sugar cube for Long Ears. I planted it in my palm and let his snout snuffle in my hand while I wrangled my emotions. *I cannot do this,* I thought. I wanted to sit down on that porch and avoid mankind all together.

But the main street of Dog Hollow bustled with people. *This is your one chance to ask them,* I told myself.

So I got to work, starting with a line of three men sitting on a bench outside the sawmill. I marched up to them like I was all business. (Though men rarely take someone of my age or stature seriously, they *will* be taken by surprise.)

The oldermost seemed to have grown on that bench, slumped some, and then stuck. A toadstool would have been more responsive to my questions. But the other two took the photograph from my hands most willingly, and peered closer when they heard my sister's hair was auburn.

The one with the pencil-thin mustache whistled.

The man next to him tittered away. "Myself? Never gone over for carroty hair. But he likes it." He pointed a dirt-encrusted finger at his friend. "You like the Garrow girl. All that Scottish red hair. But where she been? Not missing you. She's not been a-visiting." The man barked a laugh, showing a row of tiny, sharp teeth.

"Shut up," said the mustached man.

The sharp-toothed one kept on. "He notes if there's a redhead in town."

"Shut up," said the mustached man again.

I took the photo from the sharp-toothed one and put it under the other man's mustache. "Well?" I said.

"You're young to be trampousing about," interrupted Sharp Tooth.

"That's neither here nor there," I said to him before turning again to his mustached friend. "Tell me if you've seen her. Please."

The mustached man put his hand on the photograph.

"Maybe. Maybe with another woman and a man in a wagon? After the nesting broke?"

"Did you talk to her? Or did you see anyone else talk to her? Do you know where she might have gone? Or who might know?"

"I observed her. She may have talked to those people she was with. I did not speak with her."

The sharp-toothed man set to rocking back and forth, sniggering all the while. "Oh, miss, he wishes he could talk to these gals. All he can do is look. Has to *pay* for his company. If you take my meaning."

The oldermost, the toadstool, glanced over, set his jaw, and stilled.

The mustached man gave the sharp-toothed one a direct look. "I *told* you to shut up."

"I appreciate your time," I said.

I spoke with a good handful of people. Some refused to talk. One—a flush-faced woman with a rooster clamped under an arm and a stride brisk as scissors—put out a hand. "No nearer—I'm liable to snap you instead of this rooster's neck. Tonight all his cock-a-doodling becomes chicken-noodling."

Others took their time: for instance, the cowboy with as pronounced a parenthetical gait as I've ever seen. He held that photograph so long that I thought he'd fallen asleep standing up. He startled me when he handed it back. And after all that wait, what does he say? "Sure did." It took me two minutes of questioning to find out that he'd seen Agatha with the two men and one woman. When I asked where she might have gone? He pointed at the road.

Finally, I sat back down on the Dog Hollow General Store porch for a breather. I pulled out one of those licorice sticks and let the sweetness melt on my tongue.

Long Ears watched me. I glanced at him and saw him thinking, *Sugar cubes.*

"Sugar is for when you're good," I said.

Long Ears snorted, and put his muzzle back into the water trough.

Agatha had been here. She'd been noticed. People had even noticed the pigeoners with her. But that was it. They didn't seem to know anything more, like where Agatha or the pigeoners might have gone, or who else the pigeoners knew (if they did know anyone). The people in Dog Hollow had simply noticed strangers passing through town.

I needed to do better than this. Much better. If I could not have a lead on my sister's whereabouts, then—at the very least—I wanted to find something that made it *impossible* for my sister to be the body wearing that blue-green dress.

I had not done that. I had not even come close.

"Girl?" I heard from behind me.

"Girl?" I heard again. Two fingers rapped my shoulder. I shifted around from my seated position on the porch, looked up, and saw the store owner. Out in the open, she was even more impressive. I stood.

"Yes, ma'am?" I said.

"Come with me," she said. I followed her back into the store. She handed me a bottle labeled GOOD FOR WHAT AILS YOU. I read the small print:

> This powder, when mixed with water, helps disorders in the Eyes, the Coats of the Stomach, and cures all bloody Fluxes. The major ingredient comes from the dung of the hottest of all Fowls and is wonderfully attractive, yet accompanied with an Anodyne force and helps the Head-ach, Megrim, pain in the Side and Stomach, Pleurisy, Cholick, Apoplexy, Lethargy and Many other Disorders.

I met the store owner's gaze.

She started: "Your sister traveled with the man that sold me these. I believe he said his name was . . ." Here, the store owner tugged at a pile of papers spiked on a banker's stake. She sorted through them. "Metcalf?"

I glanced at the receipt and handed it back. There was nothing of note upon it, other than the name at the bottom.

The store owner nodded. "Your sister was pretty. I noticed her outside waiting in the wagon. Including your sister, there were four of them—two men and two women."

"Do you know where they went?"

"I didn't ask. He did not look like somebody that would tell me his plans."

"What do you mean by that?"

"I mean, he was the type that does a little of this and a little of that. I doubt Metcalf is his name. Your sister did not fit with those people."

"They were dangerous?"

The store owner paused before answering. "You're young. I do not want to pain you. But you came all this way. That man was the type that takes to fast, easy money. Those kinds will do anything—legal or not. People like that mix with the wrong sorts."

She set her hand on mine. "It would not surprise me if your sister came in harm's way."

It was not what I'd been hoping to hear, and I stepped onto the porch with a heavy heart.

Then I saw something. From the corner of my eye, I saw Billy McCabe coming out of the telegraph office. It was the tiniest office and barely visible from where I sat. But I saw him leave and I leapt to a conclusion. I watched him cross to the butcher shop. As soon as he stepped inside, I raced down the street to the telegraph office.

I pulled open the door and skidded to a stop in the middle of the wood floor. "Who was that telegram for? The one done by that blond boy. He just left? Tell me who he sent word to. It's urgent. Life and death!"

The door slammed shut behind me.

A tiny man, all bones and knobs, and in a mostly clean shirt, sat behind a large oak desk. To his right stood the telegraph machine. He took off his glasses, wiped the matter out of his eyes, and squinted at me. Then he set the glasses back on his nose and wrapped their wire temples around his ears one at a time.

"Your name?" His voice creaked, as if it had run out of sound like a pen will of ink.

"Show me the telegram," I said. I put my hands on his desk and leaned to read it.

A bony hand slipped the piece of paper and the logbook into a drawer. "Your name?"

"Agatha Burkhardt," I said loud and clear.

He giggled. He did! What was left of his hair bobbed about his head like some sort of angelic nimbus. "Well, Miss Agatha, you can still catch that young man if you'd like to ask him. He said he was going to the butcher's. That's what I *can* tell you. Otherwise, Western Union is not in the habit of divulging private communications." He peered over his fingertips, which he tapped together in anticipation of my next move.

"Fine," I said.

I disliked that man. I did not give him the courtesy of a good-bye.

I waited for Billy on the store porch.

When he appeared, waving a package of pork sausage over his head and asking if I'd gotten the bread and cheese, I walked at him with purpose.

I grabbed a clump of his shirt. "Who did you write a telegram to? Who was it?"

"It wasn't any secret. . . ."

"Tell me the *truth,* Billy. Did she answer you? Where is she?"

He stopped. "She? It wasn't she. It was my pa. Now let go."

My hand unclenched. His shirt fabric slipped from my fingers.

Then his eyes got wide. "Did you think I telegraphed *Agatha*?"

I stared at him.

"Agatha is dead, Fry. I thought that's why we came out here. So you'd see sense."

"I came here to *find* my sister," I said. My eyes felt damp. I could not believe this. "You sent a telegraph to your pa? Grandfather Bolte knows too, doesn't he? What *is* going on?"

He stood there, mute.

It came to me: "I asked you for a horse—paid good money too—*and* for privacy, and you went to them! All of you decided that this trip would be good for me. If I went, you *all* thought, I'd finally understand that my sister was dead." A stunned numbness overtook me.

I looked at him. "Did Ma know about this?"

Billy's chin lifted defensively. "Your grandfather was going to tell her."

"I can*not* believe it."

Billy held up his hands. "Did you think no one would

notice our absence? Your grandfather would follow you in two snaps after what happened to Agatha. I was ready to tell if you asked."

"That's less than honest," I said.

I remembered how Grandfather Bolte had cleaned both the guns—the Springfield and the double-barrel—right before we left. I remembered how he'd put the Springfield into my hands and called it a "good rifle." I *had* thought it odd that he cleaned them in June when he'd just done it in February.

I felt my strength leave me. I crossed my arms over my body, more to hold myself together than anything else. "Why'd you agree to come?"

In retrospect, I can see that I wanted him to say something about my companionable nature. Sure, the trip was a *task,* but not an onerous one, because Billy liked me. Any small hint would have done it—it would have been merely polite.

Instead, Billy said: "You approached me! I was the best choice. Come on, Fry, we all *know* you. You were resolute. Even Mr. Bolte said he didn't think he could dissuade you, not after he heard you'd offered me the Bechtler dollars."

"To force me to face the facts."

"Absolutely."

"Anything else I need to ask you so I know what you're hiding?"

"Nope."

I laid my eyes on him. "What about pay? Did Grandfather Bolte *pay* you to chaperone me?"

"Criminy, Fry."

"Tell me."

Billy puffed up his cheeks and exhaled. "Some. Yeah. For my time."

That was it for me. I turned on my heel and began to load up my mule.

"I'm sorry, Fry."

I did not answer that.

"Where are we going?" he said.

I looked over my shoulder at him. "We're going to see this spot where the body was found, remember? You're a hired hand, so I expect you to do as I say and not give me a hint of trouble. You hear me?"

"Is that the way it's going to be?"

"Are you *hired* or not?"

"I swear," said Billy.

So now I knew: Billy was not out here to meet Agatha. Money was his motive. It made too much sense for me to ignore. Weren't he and Polly planning to move to Minnesota? Homesteading is nothing if not expensive. That was why Billy was traveling with me, and why Polly Barfod would not object.

Farther on, we roasted pork sausage for dinner. Our destination was about five miles up the road, but I decided that I wanted to view that spot fresh, after I'd tried to get some sleep. I had a lot on my mind.

I questioned Billy good and hard over dinner. Billy said

that his pa, the sheriff, had tracked Agatha and the pigeoners to Dog Hollow. He figured that they were headed to Prairie du Chien, so he continued on Miller Road past Dog Hollow. When he found the body in the blue-green dress, he thought he should bring it home as quickly as possible for Ma to identify.

At this point, Billy pulled out a leather pouch that hung around his neck. He opened it and withdrew a folded piece of paper. "He gave me this."

I unfolded it and saw a crude diagram of the roadside location of each body part found. I swallowed hard and handed it back to him. "Tomorrow," I said.

Who had the sheriff talked to in Dog Hollow? He told Billy that he'd talked to several people, and though some had seen Agatha and the pigeoners, no one seemed to know much about them. They didn't know their names, or where they were headed. It seemed the pigeoners kept to themselves.

I told Billy about the Dog Hollow store owner and the bottles of medicine made from pigeon dung, and how one of the pigeoners had used the name of Metcalf. It was news to him, which meant I'd sniffed out something the sheriff had not. I felt no pride in it. It amounted to the same situation—not enough information.

I asked if Sheriff McCabe had theorized about how this all came to be.

But Billy said that his pa didn't engage in scenarios and what-ifs. "You know how Pa always says that keeping the peace is his main job. He called those pigeoners 'lazy schemers.' I don't think he considered them murderous. He *was* curious about why that body had been left out so animals could get it. But his first concern was to get the body back to your ma."

"To *identify*," I said.

Billy shrugged. "Whatever you want, Fry."

I kept company with my thoughts for the rest of that dinner. Afterward, I did my chores and Billy did his. I had momentary notions of subjecting Billy to hired-hand treatment, but as it turned out, I did not have the energy for exerting authority, and in the few days we'd traveled together, we'd developed certain routines. For instance, I cleaned the dishes, and Billy took care of our mounts. So I let that desire go.

As I was preparing for bed, Billy grabbed my elbow and looked me square in the eye. "We were saying good-bye. That was all."

It took me a moment to realize he was talking about the kiss.

"She said she was going to marry Mr. Olmstead. She wished me well. That's it. It didn't mean nothing. I never made a plan to meet her. I didn't send her a telegram. If you think she could have made all her family think she was dead . . ." He shook his head. "Agatha wasn't like that."

"You *whistled*," I said quietly.

"It didn't mean nothing."

Then he walked away.

That night I unfolded my bedroll out in the open and lay on top. *Take me.* I offered myself to any passing cougar that might want to feast on one skinny little neck. But no cougars came. Apparently, I wasn't worth dragging off. I stared up at a sky spread over with stars. Silken breezes brushed against my skin. The scent of evergreen lingered in the air. It was an irritatingly beautiful night.

I closed my eyes, and instead of counting sheep, I counted ifs: If I hadn't seen that kiss. If I hadn't told Mr. Olmstead. If I had told Agatha instead. What if I could not find her? What if there was a good reason for Agatha's tracks ending in Dog Hollow?

What if she was . . . ?

CHAPTER TWELVE

It was a nowhere place. It wasn't even in Dog Hollow. It was a half day's ride out of Dog Hollow.

As Billy and I rode the next morning, I was silent. I guess my head was working so hard there was no way to make talk too. I did worry about Long Ears taking it personally. Don't know why. He was only a mule. But for some reason, I cared, so every once in a while I'd feed Long Ears a sugar cube, which made him like me better. I wish sugar cubes worked that well with people. I'd carry them in my coat pockets, my hat, my shoes.

"Lying off the side of the road" was the only description I'd heard when people explained the location of the body.

Still, I'd imagined this place so many times that without hesitation I'd have described it as somewhere with sweeping vistas, a rock formation jutting into open air, and nearby, a knotty oak. The limbs of that oak would tangle in every direction, testifying to the struggles of wind, sun, fire, and rain, and yet there it stood, going on, full of leaves. The body, of course, would lie under this tree.

I'd like to point out that this is a sight short of what the place of someone's death should look like. People are *supposed* to die at home. They're *supposed* to have time to tell last wishes. They're *supposed* to be able to pray, to repent for their sins, and to commend their soul to God. And the family? We're *supposed* to be able to gather round the deathbed, hear those final words, watch the dying breathe their last, and witness their countenance. So given all this, I do not think the presence of a big oak tree was asking too much.

But no matter what I had imagined before, I had never imagined this: that we would pass the spot right up. This spot was *that* unremarkable. Billy figured it out—a sure miracle if there ever was one. He pulled Storm up short, took Sheriff McCabe's diagram from the pouch around his neck, studied it, and then turned around. For about a mile, we couldn't have gone any slower if we'd been strolling on foot. Finally, Billy stopped and got down off Storm.

I knew what that meant. "Are you sure?" I said.

If Billy felt any surprise at my finding my tongue, he didn't show it. Instead, he nodded and stared down at the paper. He lifted his head to gaze at a rock, then pointed at it. "See that fissure? It's the same on the diagram. This is it."

My feet felt leaden as I eased myself off Long Ears. (I still hear the scuff sound my shoes made as they hit dirt.) After that, about all I could do was keep hold of Long Ears' reins and stare about me.

This is all wrong, I thought. *Not here.* This was nowhere. Instead of being wide and generous, this was a squeezing, wrenching place, somewhere with a grip around the windpipe. It barely held a set of wagon-wheel tracks. A high hill with a rocky front formed a wall on one side, tossing shade over the road. On the other side, brambles, thistles, and tall grasses blanketed a slope leading down to the Wisconsin River. We'd passed miles and miles of road that looked like this—pass-through spaces, not stopping places.

It couldn't be here.

I can hear your thoughts. You're thinking: *See, she cares. This isn't about* some *body—this is about* Agatha's *body. It's good to see her coming round to her senses.*

Though I'd argue with you on principle. Think about it: no one should be found dead in a nowhere place— somewhere between here and there with no distinguishing marks except (like I found) a fresh pile of horse apples confettied with flies.

Now, I know people die in nowhere places. My own pa is gone. He's probably dead, and we never did find out what happened to him, let alone his last wishes. And what about Pin Eyes' brothers who died in the Civil War? Down South they're still burying bodies, and it's six years past the end of the war.

Of course, I *knew* all of this as I stood by the side of the road. But I was learning that knowing things does not mean you understand them.

Billy reached for his hat.

"Do not take off your hat," I said.

He lifted the hat off his head and brought it down to his chest. He held it there.

I let go of Long Ears' reins and started slugging Billy anywhere I could reach. "Do not take off your hat! Do not take off your hat!"

Billy pulled me toward him, pressing my face into his chest with the hat hand. The hat clapped against my back. I yelped. Under that hat, it was a dark, dark place with the sound of a shovel, then dirt and rocks striking pine boards.

My teeth found flesh and clamped down.

"Almighty!" he yelled, letting me go.

I ran up the hill on the north side of the road. I could hear his voice as I ascended. "You bit my arm? I'm bleeding." But his words were wallpaper to the sound of my feet pummeling the ground, my hands swatting back saplings, and my lungs gasping for breath.

At the top, I saw the rocks—big rocks piled high. As I tried to catch my breath, I knew that if Agatha had been anywhere nearby, she'd have climbed up here. She wouldn't have been able to resist. Agatha would have seen this place was full of hiding spots. She'd have left something here—her sketch pad or perhaps a note. Yes.

I ran over to those rocks, climbed to the highest point, and stuck my hand in a crevice all the way around the rock. Everything I touched—living or dead—I pulled out. Then I did it again and again, working my way over that entire pile of rocks. I shoved, leaning into them until they moved and I could see what lay underneath.

There was one rock I couldn't move easily. I pushed it with the palms of my hands. I pushed at it from east, north, south, and west, and then picked the most promising angle, put my back against it, and heaved.

My feet slipped and gave way. I rolled ten feet, ripping my sleeve, bruising every part of my body, and banging my cheek hard. I felt my cheek swell—heat rising in it. (No wonder my face later looked like a topographic map.)

Still, I picked myself up and sifted through what I'd collected: dead beetles and flies, decomposing leaves, twigs wrapped in old spiderwebs, a snake skin, a deserted mouse nest, live pill bugs and centipedes.

Oh! I felt something leggy run up my arm. I brushed a spider off. Then I saw another on my foot, and another on my elbow. I was brushing myself everywhere, half crying out. I quick untied my hair and shook it—dancing like a green-horn since I do not like creeping things. I saw a four-inch centipede caught in my hair. I picked it out and slung it away, stepping back at the same time. My ankle twisted. I swore.

There was not one piece of paper in all that mess—not a note, a sketch, or a scrap with a message. I had been so sure too: I'd *felt* it. I'd *known* it. Agatha would leave me something. It would be *here*. She would not leave me with nothing!

I felt everything I cared about drain from me as a result of that word: nothing. No thing. No.

My legs would not hold. I sat down.

Was I truly expecting to get to the place where the body was found and find a *note*? Maybe. Yes. All right then, I admit it. People in stories are sometimes expected to possess sterling character, to act with courageous purpose, and, on top of it all, to be a smidge smarter than everyone else. Well, maybe if I were writing my memoirs, I'd polish myself up and forget a few things. But I'm telling the entire truth now. My story, as best I can tell it, is all I have to offer.

I sat on top of that bluff. That's where I dried up and turned into jerky. It felt like that, anyway. Every bit of juice in me gone. My skin tightened and started to itch. I'm sure my lips went blue and my brown eyes took on the powdery quality of dried beans in a bag.

At first, my mind felt empty, as if a powerful wind had blown it clean. But little bits crept in: birdsong, leaves shushing in a breeze. I noticed clouds combed thin across a blue sky, and the odd red-purple boulders flecked with white. I noted that grass was greenest at the point it came out of the ground.

In Dog Hollow, I had wanted to hear something that would make me think Agatha couldn't be the body in the blue-green dress—a hint, the slightest mention, a whisper, an innuendo, anything at all. But instead, I heard that Agatha had been traveling with people of less-than-reputable character. The shopkeeper had concluded that the body on Miller Road was, indeed, Agatha.

The body wore a dress made from a bolt of cloth I'd seen in our store all summer and into the fall. I remembered running my hands over that cloth. I remembered Ma asking me if my hands were clean. That fabric was punctured by Ma's needle and thread. I could read Ma's stitching as easily as a book. *That* dress was worn by *that* body.

The body was of a young woman. The young woman had auburn hair.

The body *should* be Agatha. It would be *strange* if the body weren't Agatha. Why wouldn't the body be Agatha?

Agatha was—very likely, for the most part, probably, almost certainly, yes, surely—dead. That was a *d* at the beginning, a *d* at the end. No forward or backward. No breath either.

Why didn't she write? If she wrote one solitary letter . . . It was a thought from some younger part of me. But the voice was tiny and weak, barely a whisper. It petered to a squeak, and then was gone.

I howled.

I wasn't crying. I was *howling*—like coyotes do. That's the best I can describe it. I didn't hear it—I *was* it. I became a high-pitched whine that rose and dropped, sometimes clear in tone, and sometimes a ragged, gravelly bark. I went on like that for some time. Minutes? Hours? Who knew? I did not care.

Then I walked down the hill on legs that felt as hollow as flutes.

Billy stood in the middle of Miller Road studying the sheriff's diagram. I made my way to him, and he talked to me like I'd been there the entire time. He pointed at the rock with the fissure again. "That's the spot everything is measured from," he said.

I met his eyes and saw red in them. His face was streaked. (I couldn't help but notice a full set of teeth marks swelling on his arm.) I took a breath to steady myself, nodded, and turned my body toward the rock.

We got to work. We used Billy's strides (he's about the same height as his pa) and measured everything out. There were three spots where parts of a body had been found. At each, Billy stopped walking and said the name of what was found. He spoke so softly I asked him to repeat himself more than once.

(I'd rather not repeat those words. It was enough to see that body and, later, to hear the words for each part spoken aloud at the place where they were found. There is no one—not even you—who can force me to speak it out as well.)

Then we'd done it. We stood there for a moment and watched the river pass by. At some point, Billy looked at me. "Maybe we should search more generally," he said.

"I'll do the river," I said.

Billy nodded and turned to walk toward the hill.

I said: "You don't need to check the rocks. I did a thorough job." It was a joke, but I was many miles from a smile.

"I heard," said Billy. It was the only thing he ever said about my howl.

CHAPTER THIRTEEN

There is nothing so final as turning around.

Billy and I were back in Dog Hollow. It was noon. We were eating lunch on the banks of the Smoke River. I watched a train pull into the station and thought for the first time, *I am going home.*

We hadn't spoken the words outright. They didn't need saying. It was a foregone conclusion. There was no new evidence. Our search near the nowhere place hadn't netted a thing: Billy didn't find anything on the hillside and I didn't find anything by the river. Billy said his pa would have done a thorough search, and anyway, it was half a month since Agatha had run off. We were too late.

What could I do but go home? I'd been to the nowhere

place. I'd questioned all the people I could in Dog Hollow. There was not a thing to find.

My lunch tasted like sawdust. The bread, cheese, and dried meat were of fine enough quality, but nothing *tasted* anymore. The only thing I wanted was the one thing I could not have: my sister's companionship.

From here on out, I'd have to keep my own company. Trouble was, I didn't like myself much. In the course of this journey, I'd made an unpleasant discovery. I had discovered that I willfully deny the facts, even when the facts are arranged before me in a pine box with the lid slid off.

Then I did taste something—bitterness. I hated how Grandfather Bolte, the sheriff, and Billy had used my plan to fashion their own. Worse, I hated how well it had worked: I *had* come around. I'd seen the light. Hallelujah, my sister was dead.

"Agatha is dead," I called out. I threw a crust at the river passing beyond my feet. "Isn't that what you want to hear? I am going home changed. I am a girl with a palatable attitude."

To his credit, Billy did not reply. He simply bit off another hunk of bread.

After four or five feet of river had ambled by, Billy reached out and touched my cheekbone. "None of my brothers ever managed one that good. Does it hurt?"

"Now that you mention it," I said. I had noticed the heat gathering around my cheekbone. My left eye had difficulty opening. Billy's fingers on my face caused the most pleasant feeling I'd had in hours. When he ran his hand through my hair, sorting it out in a most caring manner, I could not meet his eyes.

I knew Billy was only doing what he'd do for his younger brothers. "You're a mess. You should clean yourself up while I put lunch away," he said. He stood.

I grabbed his forearm. "I murdered her. If I hadn't told Mr. Olmstead . . ."

Billy turned quickly. "*Don't.* I'm warning you."

"I know I didn't shoot her. But if I had let it be. Or talked to Agatha. Or done anything other than talk to Mr. Olmstead . . ."

Billy gripped my shoulder and squeezed *hard*. "I will not listen to this. Clean yourself up. We're going home."

Billy let go and, without a backward glance, walked toward our mounts.

His anger hushed me. Perhaps he was right. Who could endure listening? I felt ashamed. I resolved to be made of sterner stuff.

My reflection alarmed me (and I'm not one to set store by appearances). Nearly everything on the left side of my face blazed blue, purple, and red, like leadplant in full bloom. My left eye was swelling shut. I put my hand on it tentatively. The rest of me wasn't much better: ripped and soiled clothing, bits of everything trapped in my hair. I splashed river water on my banged-up face and on the sullied parts of my clothing.

My hands shook, so it took double the time to undo my hair and braid it up again.

As I did this, all that I had found out about Agatha bobbled vaguely in my mind. Suddenly I realized something—something that I had not asked about. I needed to do it. Right now.

I marched past Billy, who stood by our mounts.

Billy mentioned getting going.

I held out my hand. "Give me a moment. Wait here," I said.

I did not mean to push open the door to the Dog Hollow General Store with such force, but I did enter with a purposeful momentum. That door hit the wall and rattled.

"You," came her voice. "What happened to your face?"

I saw the owner slowly stand upright. I walked to the counter, talking as I went. "Those people with my sister—the ones that sold you the quack cures—"

"I observed their beneficial effects myself," she said quickly.

"The medicines—yes," I said, putting my hand on the counter. "Where do you think the pigeoners went *after* they sold those bottles to you? I work at a store too. We know where people tend to go. We get an idea of who consorts with who, even if we're not told outright. You can't own a store and not know what's what."

Her eyes narrowed. "That man was completely unknown to me."

"I'm sure you can guess. Those people that sell medicines and the like travel on a circuit. They buy something here, sell it over there. If those pigeoners were to buy something to sell, who would they buy from? You *told* me you *hear* things."

"You think that man gave me his confidence? He didn't say more than a dozen words."

"But what about a person *like* him? Someone that straddles the fence of legality."

She looked at me close. "You are begging for trouble. Have you seen your face? Yesterday you looked like a girl. Today you look like ..." She did not finish her sentence. "Young miss, you should walk out of this store right now."

"There is no rest until this is settled. I *will* endure anything." I gestured at the one thing that seemed to be moving her—my face.

The store owner sighed. "You must give your word not to mention my name. Or my store."

"I give my word," I said.

"The Garrows. Up on the bluff. I don't know what they do, or what they sell. I don't *want* to know. But people of certain reputations seem to be acquaintances of the Garrows. Those people traveling with your sister were the type."

I asked for directions.

Billy thought I'd lost my mind. He screwed his hat on. "Fry, your *ma* stitched the dress found on the body."

"It's only a half day out of the way. Isn't *half* a day worth

140

it? The Garrows may know where those pigeoners went. Think of it as tying up loose ends."

He locked his eyes on me. "Your sister was *shot*."

"I won't accuse them! I'll ask if the pigeoners have been there and which way they went. I will not bring my sister up at all."

"No."

"If we do not find anything, I will go home willingly. I can't take much more anyway. I'm wrung out."

Billy adjusted his stance.

"It will *only* take *half* a day."

Billy crooked a finger at me. "You're not harboring any notion that your sister is alive, are you? Tell me now: Is Agatha dead or alive?"

"She's dead," I said.

Finger jab. "After this we head home?"

"Yes sir."

"A half day out of the way?"

"That's all I need," I said.

We stopped by the telegraph office. The telegram read: "At DH. Garrow lead, then home. Billy."

CHAPTER FOURTEEN

The store owner had described the Garrows as people who kept to themselves on a land "riddled with rocks and caves." I thought about those rocks and caves as we rode away from Dog Hollow and into the bluffs that embraced the Wisconsin River. It was a landscape Agatha would relish, which sparked hope that Agatha was indeed alive. I knew this was a silliness. It was like what I'd done at the nowhere place when I'd pushed aside rocks to look for notes. I will also admit that when I considered going home, I imagined a letter waiting. This was my third day gone—a letter *could* arrive in three days. It was hopeless because surely Agatha was dead. Yet I persisted in thinking these things, hoping where I should not hope.

What was I doing going up to the Garrows'? Wasn't this like all the others—an acting out of a fanciful hope?

But I was determined to go. I said to myself: *Only half a day out of my way.* Or: *Dead or not, I will never rest easily until I know what happened.* Or: *If this amounts to nothing, I will go home.*

We would travel eight miles northeast on a mostly unused road known as Old Line. There we'd find Garrow Farm. Upon concluding our visit, we could continue on Old Line over the top of the bluff, following it until it joined up with Miller Road, our route home. The store owner had stressed that past Garrow Farm, Old Line wouldn't be much more than a footpath since the road hadn't been used in twenty-odd years. But on horseback we should be able to follow what was left of it, and this shortcut would save us several hours of travel. We were essentially heading home (albeit in a roundabout manner).

It was two o'clock by the time we got started. The clouds stretched tight across the sky, and the hot stuck to me. My head felt like it might split, ripening under all that heat. The bruise pounded out its own rhythm. I assumed that by night-fall my left eye would be shut entirely.

In general, Old Line Road wasn't much. A table-flat boulder piled with rocks marked the turnoff, and after that we followed two spindly wagon tracks straight up into the hills. (Hills on the lower Wisconsin River push out of the ground for no discernible reason, and Old Line seemed determined to traverse them.)

The state of that road gave me pause. It was in no shape

for wagons: boulders and rocks studded the route; gullies and trenches ripped through it; and good-sized seedlings sprouted between the two ruts. Obviously, someone had dragged a wagon over that land, but I could not imagine who'd be fool enough to do it.

In addition, it was an uncomfortable ride. Those steep hills trapped bloodsuckers. We dipped down into two valleys foggy with mosquitoes. The mosquitoes blanketed us upon arrival, biting even Long Ears, who nipped at his hide. I smashed them for several minutes and then gave up, letting them feast, reasoning that they'd bring down the swelling of my eye. (They didn't. Instead, they made my face itch and lump up like dried oatmeal.)

Four hours later we arrived at a fence with a wagon wheel leaning against it. According to the store owner, this was Garrow Farm. The sun hung low in the sky. It was now six o'clock.

"Wait here," said Billy. He clucked his tongue at Storm.

"If you go, I go. If anything, *you* should wait here. This is *my* journey. She was *my* sister," I said. I nudged Long Ears.

Billy pulled Storm short. "We need to make a good impression. Fry, you look ..." He made some abstract hand motions, my appearance seemingly too much for his descriptive abilities. He decided to try anyway: "You're wrinkled and dirty. Your hair ... Your face—it's *orange*. They're going to think I beat you. You cannot make a call looking like you do."

I was having none of it. "Clean me up!" I said. "I am not waiting out here, and we are far from a hand mirror. May I remind you that as soon as you get out of sight, Long Ears will trot to his true love—Storm? I don't have the will to stop him."

Billy sighed. "You will not talk. Agatha will not be mentioned. Then we go home."

"Yes. I agree."

"Get out your hairbrush."

That was how Billy McCabe came to clean me up. His hairbrushing was rough and his spit-cleaning unbearable, and Billy did not know how to braid hair (four younger brothers), so I did that. After I passed inspection—barely—Billy unlatched the gate and we walked our mounts through.

It wasn't a place I'd have chosen to live. Garrow Farm was buried in a hollow on the back side of the hill. Sure, it was a fine clearing, but if you sat on the porch of the Garrows' frame house, about all you'd see was the field in terraces, cupping the house on three sides. Mr. Garrow had set his farm on a slope *away* from the Wisconsin River. And practically speaking, where they were—way up the hill—was far from water and the best soil (which lay all around them on the lowlands). If I were going to be impractical and live on top of a steep hill, I'd *at least* want a view of the river.

And imagine the work in terraced fields! Stones had been brought up on the hillside to make the terrace walls, and then crops laid in so they ringed the hills in earthen steps.

It was one of the tidiest fields I'd seen, and the prettiest too, especially with the gold light of early evening dusting those crops. But I would guess it was subsistence farming. I didn't see much to sell.

Yet somehow, the Garrows did all right. The frame house was two stories, with a wide stone chimney and a recently repaired roof. Mind you, it wasn't a palace—the porch leaned appreciably—but it looked as nice as any house I'd seen in Dog Hollow.

As we walked down their road, I saw a well for water and clothes billowing on a line. A basket sat on the ground.

A tiny girl with hair as red as a copper penny darted out from behind the house and ran to the line. She spotted us and stopped, frozen, one hand suspending a wet shirt above the basket.

She dropped the clothing. "Ma! Ma!" The girl ran back, disappearing behind the house.

We stopped.

Carroty hair, I thought. Never liked that phrase. It was common and lacked specificity. People tossed it about willy-nilly to describe red hair. Whenever someone had used it to describe Agatha's auburn hair—the color so pretty it made you ache to look at it—I had thought less of them.

But recently someone had used that term. Who was it? In my mind, I saw those three men—the sharp-toothed, the mustached, and the oldermost—sitting on the bench outside the sawmill. Hadn't the sharp-toothed one said "the Garrow girl"? They'd been discussing this family—I was sure of it. Funny how we'd ended up here.

Billy gave me a quick smile and removed his hat.

A moment later, a woman about the size of a fifteen-year-old boy with straight hips and a plain walk appeared. The tiny girl ran behind her and wrapped herself around the woman's leg. The woman stopped, then disentangled the girl and gave her a shove toward the house. She shaded her eyes in our direction and strode toward us.

A useful woman—that's what Ma would say. There wasn't one ounce of waste on her, everything toughened and wiry. I didn't doubt that she'd built these terraces herself. She didn't look done in either, like most of the homesteading women that came into our store. This woman knew where to spend her strength. I admired that. I found I wanted her to like me. But friendship was out of the question: it was clear by the directness of her gaze that we were idling away the last of her daylight.

"Mrs. Garrow?" said Billy.

The woman lifted her chin up.

A door slammed. I glanced at the house and saw that the tiny girl was gone.

"I'm Billy and this is Georgie," Billy said.

Mrs. Garrow took a long look at my face. When Billy offered his hand, Mrs. Garrow did not take it.

Billy continued unabashed. His voice was so honey-thick I could have spread it on bread. I knew his charm wouldn't work, but it was too late to stop him. "We're trying to find some pigeoners coming from Placid. Their name may have been Metcalf. They traveled through this area about three weeks ago. Have you seen them?"

"Never *heard* of them. Now, I don't mean to be rude, but I got work. Good day," she said. She turned to go.

Billy tapped his hat against the side of his thigh, then called out: "What about a young lady with auburn hair about eighteen years of age?"

We'd agreed not to speak of Agatha. I stared at Billy.

Billy opened his hands wide, indicating that he didn't know what else to do.

Mrs. Garrow turned abruptly. "If you're talking about my eldest daughter, Darlene, she's gone. She eloped with her beau, Morgy Harrison, of Owatonia. And no, I don't know when she'll be back. They've gone off and gotten married, so there's no use in you holding out any hope. Now, I know my Darlene has plenty of followers, but it does beat all when someone comes in here and asks after my daughter accompanied by a young girl so obviously struck in the face."

"I fell," I said quickly. Meanwhile, my mind reeled. Had Mrs. Garrow said what I thought she had said? Had *another* auburn-haired girl gone missing?

Mrs. Garrow smiled slightly. "Yes, girls who 'fall' always seem to be with sweet-talkers," she said.

I stepped away from Billy so he wouldn't put his hand on my shoulder like he was about to do (Mrs. Garrow wouldn't like that), and said what I desperately needed to say: "When did Darlene leave?"

"A couple of weeks ago." Then Mrs. Garrow gestured at the fields. "She left me with all this work. Slips off without leaving a note. I heard from the Harrisons that the two of them eloped. My husband says he gave his blessing. Gives his blessing!"

I barely listened. Two girls missing around the same time and from the same general vicinity: this Garrow girl lived outside of Dog Hollow, and my sister disappeared from somewhere around Dog Hollow.

Mrs. Garrow paused, then said: "Listen to me. I don't normally chatter on like this."

A wild idea had taken root in my head. I hardly dared to hope it. Still, the only way it *could have* happened was if Agatha had given the blue-green dress to Darlene. I reached into one of the saddlebags for the photograph of Agatha.

I held it out to Mrs. Garrow and said: "I *am* sorry to hear how Darlene left you like she did, but Billy was describing my *sister,* not your daughter. Have you seen my sister? Her name is Agatha Burkhardt." As Mrs. Garrow took the photograph, I added: "Is there any chance Darlene might have met her?"

Billy exhaled, and I knew he understood where I was going.

Mrs. Garrow looked at the image. "I've never seen this girl. Darlene hardly ever leaves the farm. I keep her busy."

"You lost?" a voice called out.

I looked over and saw a bear of a man with a barrel chest and a woolly rust-colored beard push out the front door with a pitcher and two tin cups. Three children followed in his wake. I noted all the red hair: there was the tiny girl (copper hair), one arm latched around a porch pillar; the next tallest, a strawberry-blond boy maybe a year older standing in the center of the porch; and finally, an even older rusty-haired boy who had dropped to the porch's edge to sit.

The man came toward us holding out the pitcher. "Quite a trip up here. Must be thirsty. I'm Mr. Blair Garrow. I see you've met my wife," he said. He smiled all the way to his hairline. We couldn't help but smile in return as we introduced ourselves.

But before Mr. Garrow could give us cups and pour the water, Mrs. Garrow put her hand on his forearm. "These people want to know if we've seen three pigeoners by the name of Metcalf traveling with this girl."

Mrs. Garrow handed her husband the photograph. She continued: "They're wondering if Darlene met her."

As Mr. Garrow glanced at the photograph, I thought I saw something pass over his face. I didn't know what it was, though. A thought? A recognition?

He shook his head. "No. Never seen her. You searching for her?" Mr. Garrow looked briefly at his wife, then handed the photograph to Billy, who passed it on to me.

"We are," said Billy.

"Never heard of any of them. Except my daughter, of

course. Wish I could help." He paused and said: "Well, sun's going down. Don't want to keep you." He held up the pitcher. "Water for your canteens?"

Billy shook his head. "Appreciate it, but we filled them in Dog Hollow."

He pointed at me. "That's quite a mouse on your eye."

I nodded, thinking it best not to say any more.

Mrs. Garrow gave Billy a piercing look. "She's no more than eleven. Shame on you," she said. She left without saying good-bye.

Billy turned bright red. (I did not think I looked *that* young.)

Mr. Garrow sighed. "She means well." He patted Billy on the shoulder. "You'll have to get going if you want to make it out of these hills by nightfall."

"Old Line goes over the hill and joins up with Miller Road?" said Billy.

"There's no road that way anymore. The only road is the one you came in on. Good night, now." Then he also turned to walk to the house.

As I tucked Agatha's photograph in a saddlebag, I saw that the tiny girl had snuck up behind me to get close to Long Ears. She leaned against his muzzle like he was some sort of puppy. Why that mule allowed it, I did not know, but other than snapping his tail, Long Ears seemed unperturbed.

The girl peered at me from the other side of Long Ears' head. "Did you hurt yourself?"

I touched my face. The skin felt stretched, hard, and bloated. "I slipped on some rocks."

"Oh," said the girl. She came out from behind Long Ears' head to where I stood. "I admire donkeys. My pa says I can get one as a pet."

"It's a *mule*," I said irritably. I did not care for my mount being referred to as a pet. Especially by a girl less than half my size, with not a tenth of my vocabulary.

"What's a mule?" she said.

"Never mind," I said. No one wants to explain the origin of mules to small children.

The tiny girl wasn't listening anyway. She stretched up to try to bend one of the mule's ears down so that she could stroke it. Being unsuccessful with the ear (too small to reach it), she covered Long Ears' velvety snout in kisses. Long Ears snorted and backed away, finally drawing his proverbial line in the sand.

Billy had mounted and started off. Long Ears now wanted to go too. He stomped.

And then I saw it in the tiny girl's hair. I saw a most unusual shade of blue green.

"Do you like black licorice sticks?" I said quickly, unbuckling the nearest saddlebag.

"Yes!" Her hands fell from Long Ears' face. She hopped right beside me.

I held the licorice stick out away from the girl and put my other hand on one end of that blue-green ribbon. As the tiny girl leaned to take the licorice, the bow in her copper hair came undone and the ribbon fell away. I balled the ribbon up, hiding it in my palm, and mounted Long Ears.

Even when her hair tumbled to her shoulders, the tiny girl didn't notice the ribbon was gone. She was too busy sucking that licorice stick.

CHAPTER FIFTEEN

I wonder how many significant decisions in the course of history have been made because of mosquitoes. Billy and I made a decision that way. We decided we could not fathom sacrificing our bodies to the fog of mosquitoes floating in those valleys. So we did not go back the way we came, as Mr. Garrow had advised. Instead, we went up the bluff. We took the store owner's advice and followed the remains of Old Line Road. Along the way we hoped to find a flat stretch of ground to lie upon. Honestly, I barely remember discussing the topic—the decision felt *that* insignificant.

Past Garrow Farm, Old Line worsened in a hurry. It narrowed as it wound around the bluff. Trees pressed in, and fully grown bushes and brambles lined the ridge between the wagon tracks. We squeezed through, the branches slapping my legs and the barbs snagging my clothing.

Still, there's always a rut where wheels have rolled. Though after what Mr. Garrow had said, I wondered if this road would abandon us, wearing away at the top of the bluff. Fortunately, it did not.

While we rode in the usual formation—Billy and Storm ahead, Long Ears and I following—I pulled out the blue-green ribbon. In the honey light of the setting sun, I observed the row of stitches. It was a homemade ribbon. I rubbed it between my fingers and stared at it some more. For all the world, this ribbon appeared to be made from the same material as Agatha's dress. Was my sister *alive*? A thousand tiny hopes swarmed over me like a cloud of gnats.

All that hope nearly did me in. I had no endurance for it. I stuffed the ribbon into a saddlebag. I was so, so tired. From my saddle, I watched the shadows lengthen and tried not to think about *any* of the day's happenings. The bruise on my face had finally succeeded in closing my left eye, and seeing one-eyed made me dizzy. Between tiredness and dizziness, I knew it would be a joy to go to sleep.

I do think there is a limit to how much a person can feel and think on one particular day. I'd been to the nowhere place and come to the realization that my sister was dead. I'd been ready to go home. Now? I didn't know what I thought or what I wanted.

Finally, the last of the sunlight slipped over our heads,

lavender evening came upon us, and we arrived at a wide, grassy spot with purple-gray boulders to lean against. Through my right eye, I could see where the fire pit should go and where I would unroll my bed. The river sprawled below, slipping by sand islands. Behind the open area was a bald, rocky hill that climbed maybe forty feet, and then the forest took over, thick as a lumberjack's beard. I felt irked with Mr. Garrow for not mentioning this spot, but the irritation passed because *finally* the day was at its end. Billy and I dismounted, hobbled Storm and Long Ears, and set up camp without a word.

Seeing how we ate quickly and in silence, I think both of us were spent. I remember pressing my finger against the plate to dab up the last of the jam and then wiping my hands on the split skirt. I felt a tingle and found a tick winding its way up my shin. I flicked it into the fire and watched half amazed as it crawled right out. I swear those things are made of iron. I grabbed a twig, put the hot-to-the-touch tick on the end of it, and pushed the end into some embers. The end of the twig burst into flame. I pulled the twig out of the fire and examined it. When I looked up, I saw Billy watching me.

"A tick," I explained. It embarrassed me to have Billy observe me being cruel (even to a tick).

I threw the twig into the fire, looked at him, and said what I was thinking: "I want to go back to the Garrows'."

Billy nodded. "Yeah, that confusion between Darlene Garrow and Agatha would make anyone want to go back. There's two young ladies with auburn hair gone from home, and a *pack* of red-haired kids at that farm. I started wondering if Agatha might be alive. First time I *ever* thought that."

"Mr. Garrow recognized the photograph too," I said.

"Huh. I couldn't tell."

"I read something in his face. I'm not sure what, though. Not fear, or anger—which is what I'd expect if he shot Agatha. And if he recognized her—saw her someplace—why wouldn't he say so?" I paused for a moment, trying to remember the look on Mr. Garrow's face. Finally, I had it. "He looked *confused*. Why would Mr. Garrow be confused?"

Billy shook his head. "Who knows." Then he chuckled. "Asking about whether Darlene and Agatha had met was quick thinking."

I liked that he'd noticed and said so.

Billy observed me for a moment.

"I need to show you something," I said quickly. I got up and dug in the saddlebags. I brought the blue-green ribbon back to Billy. I told him how I got it.

Billy leaned forward and held the ribbon up to the light of the fire. He looked at me. "Do you think this is the same fabric?"

"I can't be sure. No one remembers colors exactly without a sample. But my instincts tell me it is. It's too similar, and Agatha's dress was made of fabric Ma ordered from Boston. It isn't a fabric that makes its way to Wisconsin all that easily."

Billy whistled low. "If this is made from Agatha's dress, how did it come to be in that little girl's hair?"

"Exactly," I said.

Billy turned it over in his hand, then gave it back to me. He shrugged. "They could have cut it off the body—salvaged a piece."

I frowned, unable to dismiss the ribbon as Billy seemed to have done. "I need to go back. I need to ask about this ribbon."

Billy pushed his hat up. "No, Fry. This is as far as we're going to pursue it. We're going home now."

I met his eyes. "What'll it hurt?"

"Remember what happened to Agatha? If those people are at all connected with that, you and I are not enough. We'd need a posse."

"We'll wait until Mrs. Garrow is alone."

Billy put his hands out. "Hold it right there, Fry. Yes, this is odd—I readily admit it. Another girl with auburn hair gone? And from a household where a similar fabric was found? But we're not returning."

Then Billy stopped and looked down at his hands. "I understand, Fry. I do. There were moments—back there—when I thought her alive."

He raised his head and looked me squarely in the eye. "You have no idea how much I want her to be alive."

He exhaled and continued: "But hope muddies up reason. Think about this *reasonably*. First, how could Agatha and Darlene meet? It would be the chanciest of chance meetings. Her ma said Darlene didn't leave their hilltop much at all. Also, we'd have to believe that Agatha sold or gave away her dress. You and I both know she thought the world of it. And then there's the problem of Darlene eloping with this Morgy. That's *two* people gone missing, which means *two* families are saying that their children eloped in secret. The elopement makes sense to those families. Sure, they're angry, but they're not worried. And two people traveling together don't come to trouble as quick as one." He shook his head. "When I think about Agatha going off alone and endangering herself . . ."

His eyes met mine again. "*One* body was found—a body wearing your sister's dress. This ribbon? Probably a coincidence. But even if your hunch is correct, it's most likely that you'd be discovering only what happened before—or after— Agatha died. Does before or after truly make any difference to you? Is it worth getting shot at? Your sister, Agatha, is *dead*."

Without warning, he scooted around so that his back was to the fire and put his head between his knees. I heard a half-strangled sound and then Billy began to sob.

I fidgeted for a moment. People don't come to me for comfort and consolation. I don't know why. They don't, is all. But it had led me to conclude that I had no talent for it. Right then, though? I was it. *Buck up,* I said to myself. I went over, sat down next to him, and laid my hand on his shoulder (like I'd seen others do).

"I can't get her back," he said into his knees.

"Uh-huh," I mumbled in my best imitation of a soothing tone.

I sat there, patting his shoulder awkwardly, and in the meantime, two things became clear to me. First, no matter what he'd said to the contrary, Billy McCabe could not marry Polly Barfod. Billy was in love with my sister. He'd need *time* to ease the pain.

The second? Tomorrow I would leave Billy. I had my Bechtler gold dollar coins (reflexively my fingers brushed the five lumps beneath the split skirt's waistband). I could also travel wherever I wanted. Long Ears listened to me now. I'd learned to speak the language of sugar cubes.

Tonight I needed sleep. But tomorrow morning I'd be awaiting my chance. I imagined that sometime midmorning, when Billy and Storm got so far ahead I could barely see them, I'd make my move. Long Ears and I would go back the way we'd come—back to the Garrows'. By the time Billy realized I was gone, I'd have an hour's head start. At that point, Billy could choose to follow me or go home. I did not care. I'd get my chance to talk to Mrs. Garrow. I *had* to find out about the ribbon.

Billy wiped his nose on his sleeve, and gave me a little grin. I smiled back, stood up, and went to my seat on the other side of the fire.

When I sat down, I said it like I meant it: "Let's go home."

"You mean it?" he said, turning around.

For better or worse, one skill I've acquired by growing up

in a store is the ability to sell. I am not proud of what I did that night, but at the time I thought I needed to convince Billy that I wanted to go home, and I *sold* him on it: "Yes. It *is* crazy that there's this other redheaded girl gone, and that there's this ribbon, but it is not enough to suggest that my sister might be alive. As you said yourself, this Darlene Garrow situation involves two people—not one. I think Mrs. Garrow told us the truth about that. So I say we remember all of this, and when we get home, we'll tell your pa. We'll see what he makes of it."

I did feel bad about lying so baldly, but if Billy suspected I had any intention of going back, he would keep an eye on me.

Billy nodded. "Good. We're going home."

I stole a glance at Billy then. The firelight played on the underside of his hat, and along the side of his jaw where his beard started in.

Billy caught me watching, and smiled.

I looked away.

Billy chuckled. "You found out more than Pa did. I'm sure of it."

I blinked.

Billy continued: "Pa would be the first to say it. If Pa had found any connection between the pigeoners and the Garrows, he would have told me. And removing that ribbon like you did? Using the licorice stick? That was smart."

Was Billy McCabe complimenting me again? I grinned.

Billy grinned back. "*And* you did a job on your face. I've never seen a bruise so encompassing."

I put my hand to my cheek. The heat pounded. My left eye was now swelled tight. "There's an entire marching band inside my head."

"I bet."

Feeling bolder, I let my one open eye linger on Billy, sipping him in, taking my time. Yes, he was well made. I would give him that. I thought about how we'd walked side by side into Garrow Farm, how he'd made me laugh, and how I made him laugh too. I thought about how I had known him all my life. He called me smart! I was wrong about Billy McCabe. He wasn't half bad. And before I knew it, I said: "You can't marry Polly. You're still in love with my sister. Maybe you should wait it out. Maybe if you waited *long enough,* someone like *me* would come along."

Had I said that out loud? My breath went shallow. Of course, I regretted it.

Billy's eyes got wide. This was swiftly replaced by that amused twinkle. After much exertion to contain himself, Billy said: "That's sweet, Fry. But I need to start my life now. I'm gonna marry Polly. I didn't mean what I said about using Polly to bring Agatha around. I've got a temper. You made me mad and I said it, but it's not true. Not anymore, anyway. I love Polly. Polly'll be a fine wife for me. Better than I deserve."

It was a misery sitting there listening to him defend Polly. What *had* I been thinking?

And had Billy called me *sweet*?

Billy smiled one of those smiles and said: "You are, by far, the best part of this journey."

"Oh," I said. It was all I could manage.

I felt utter gratitude when Billy asked for "that book" I'd brought along. I never moved so quick! I pulled *The Prairie Traveler* out of my saddlebag and handed it to him. Billy opened the book, shifting so firelight illuminated the page.

"You didn't tell me this was written by a captain of the U.S. Army," he said. I saw he'd turned to the back of the book to read the biography.

"You didn't ask," I said.

He didn't look up from the book as he replied: "There is no peace with you, is there, Fry?"

I could have answered, but why? Anyway, it seemed he was already deep in that book. I stood up and brushed off my split skirt. "I'm going to climb this hill. Come after me in fifteen minutes if I don't return," I said.

Billy paid me no mind, which was fine by me.

Yes, I would have slept if I could. But my heart raced. I do not propose marriage every day.

The half-light made those forty feet an easy climb, but my puffy, closed left eye did not. More than once I had to use my hands to steady myself. After five minutes of struggle, I reached the top, turned around, surveyed the view (impressive), and noted that Billy was *still* reading. I had never taken

Billy McCabe for a reader, but he was engrossed in *The Prairie Traveler*. So I decided to explore the back side of the hill. Not a natural choice for a walk—it was thick with brambles, bushes, and tall trees—but I found a tiny path and followed it down.

The moon came out, and moonlight reminded me of cougars' eyes. The hairs on the back of my neck rose to alert. I heard something snap.

I swung around, and when I put my right foot down, the entire ground gave way.

Down I went—bump, bump, bump—with a whole lot of tree branches and rubbish. New aches piled on old pains. I grasped at anything at all—rocky walls, moss, dirt, and pine boards. (*Pine boards?*) I stopped suddenly and heard my last thump echo. Damp air brushed my face. It smelled musty.

A cave.

Dark as an inkwell too. Agatha may like the muscle and bones of the earth, but I prefer the skin. Sky above and grass below is my motto. I won't even go into a root cellar willingly! My hand skimmed one of the sharp corners I'd bumped against and I realized it was a stair. Stairs? In a cave?

I didn't know what this place was or why people spent time in it but I wanted out. My right hand lay on something papery. I ripped it in my effort to get standing, and scrambled up those stairs as quickly as I could go.

By the time I made it back, I was truly exhausted. I plopped down in front of that fire and realized my right hand was in a fist. I opened up my hand and stared at what I held.

Billy didn't even look up. He'd heard my arrival, though. "Listen to this," he said. Then he read:

> The same Indian mentioned that when a bear had been pursued and sought shelter in a cave, he had often endeavored to eject him with smoke, but that the bear would advance to the mouth of the cave, where the fire was burning, and put it out with his paws, then retreat into the cave again.

"Now, how could that be?" Billy gestured at the book like he could convince letters to rearrange themselves into something more reasonable. "No bear does that!"

When I didn't say anything at all—no comment, no "Uh-huh," no laughter—Billy finally looked up. He squinted at me. "Again? Oh no, Fry. What kind of mess have you gotten yourself into this time?" he said. Then I saw him look at what I held in my hand. "Where did you get a five-dollar note?"

I looked down again at what I held and frowned.

"In a cave," I said.

CHAPTER SIXTEEN

Where do five-dollar banknotes come from? Five-dollar banknotes grow inside caves, right at the point where rough-hewn pine stairs meet rocky floor. They are found bound up in stacks and tossed amidst dirt, dried leaves, and tree limbs (debris left from an earlier bruise-rendering entry).

I know this because Billy made up a torch and I led him to that cave. Billy shoved aside the remaining branches with his right foot, and without so much as a "Here we go," Billy plunged down those steps into pitch blackness. I watched the torchlight ring the sides of that cave and swore Billy was walking into someone's oversized gullet.

As soon as the torchlight left, night closed in behind me and I thought, *Cougars.* So gullet or not, I scampered down the steps after that light.

Moments later I was where I'd been. There lay several bundles of five-dollar bills. The paper collar on one of the bundles was ripped. The dollars were splayed out and scattered across the ground.

No one keeps money in caves. It's either the mattress or the bank. We have a currency shortage in Wisconsin, but looking at the amount of paper money in this cave, a body would never know it.

I saw Billy inspecting another pile of banknotes. "*One-dollar notes,*" he called. He picked up a bundle and ran his thumb over the edge.

Then he stood up. He held the torch against the dark, and light illuminated the space.

Nausea slammed into me. It was a cave all right—as big as a ballroom, but lacking a ballroom's regular angles. There's no pretending a cave is a proper room—it's the belly of the whale, the innards of a clam, a bubble, a rock-hard belch. Everything is poured out and dried sideways or upside down. To my right, several columns of slick rock seemed to drip upward. There were knobby clusters, columns looking like gigantic candle-wax drippings, and a wall that folded in on itself. The torchlight wavered and shadows stretched until Billy turned and the light jerked to another spot. A fissure in a nearby wall caused me to consider that trees grew out of the cave's ceiling—which is so dadgum wrong (not to mention *heavy*).

I escaped suffocating sensations by sitting on the last pine step and focusing on roomlike elements. I saw a stool, a table covered with an oilcloth, and, on the floor, squarish mounds under tarps. I concentrated on their regular angles.

Out of the corner of my eye, I watched Billy make his way to the farthest point. He held out his torch to light a dark hole. In chorus, mouths screeched.

I screamed and dropped to the cave floor as bats swept over my head and up the stairs.

"My apologies," called Billy.

I crawled back to the step and sat down again.

Billy moved into the middle of the chamber. He lifted the torch high above his head with his left hand. With his right, he took hold of a corner of a tarp covering one of the squarish mounds and pulled. The tarp snapped and hung in the air a moment before whirling to the ground. Billy pulled another and another and another.

Agatha spinning in Billy's arms, the skirt of her blue-green dress snapping in the air with every turn around the Olmstead Hotel's ballroom.

The New Year's ball was only five months ago. It felt like decades, but truly, it was the shortest amount of time.

I began a countdown in my head. Four months ago (February), Billy had proposed marriage to Agatha. Three months ago (March), the pigeons had migrated over Placid, and Agatha had spun underneath them. Two months ago (April), Mr. Olmstead and Agatha had courted, and the pigeons had nested. One month ago (May), Agatha had kissed Billy, and the nesting had broken, along with Agatha's ties to Mr.

Olmstead. Agatha had been angry with me, but I'd honestly thought—and I hesitate to admit this—that it was all over. Life would return to the way it had been previously. Agatha would have no other choice but to run the store with me. So only one month ago, I'd felt *relieved*.

But Agatha had run off nineteen days ago. Six days ago, my family had held my sister's funeral.

Seemed like I'd lived two lifetimes already. My first thirteen years took an uneventful forever, but this second lifetime? Why, it took all of three days: Billy and I had left on a Saturday night. I'd met a cougar on Sunday. I'd been in Dog Hollow on Monday. And today was Tuesday. On Tuesday, I'd been to the nowhere place and Garrow Farm, made a marriage proposal, and found money in a cave. Would this Tuesday *never* end?

But Tuesdays end when they will and not a moment before. I squinted at what Billy was uncovering. Then, frustrated by how little I could see from my seat on the stairs, I took a few unsteady steps around the chamber. I saw a stack of paper, and a paper cutter. What had looked like a table was, in actuality, a printing press.

"Fry, come see this," said Billy. He held the torch up.

I put my hands against the wall—a bulging, earthy wall that caused my stomach to turn over—and made my way to him.

I saw it: four printing plates. I squatted and turned one over. What I saw was the reverse image of a one-dollar banknote.

I ran my hand over the engraving. "How do they make this? It's so detailed."

"They get an engraver. Or one of them is the engraver. You'd have to be an artist to produce anything like that. If they bought it, it cost them two legs and an arm. All I know is that if you want to catch a counterfeiter, you've got to catch him with the plates. Counterfeiting plates are a find. Pa would sure appreciate this."

"Mr. Garrow is a counterfeiter?" I said. It was all coming together.

"Looks like it."

"Remember how he said there was no road up this way? He didn't want us up here," I said.

Billy frowned. "But were those pigeoners also counterfeiters?"

I do believe Grandfather Bolte would have been proud of my deduction. It takes one business owner to understand another (legal or not). "No," I said slowly. "If those pigeoners met Mr. Garrow, they met him to *purchase* false notes. Mr. Garrow probably sold the notes at some percentage of the face value. Maybe forty percent? A one-dollar note would cost the pigeoners forty cents. That way, Mr. Garrow didn't have to risk passing false notes himself. He'd still make plenty of money."

Billy looked at me with genuine admiration. "I swear, Fry."

"I *do* work on the account books at the store. It's not all scrubbing pigeon defecation," I said. Some people think that my youthful age precludes me from responsibility. It is irksome.

Billy did not respond to my fit of pique. Instead, he stood upright with a jerk. "We've got to get out of here. We've got to put out that fire. We have to clean this place up, and our camp too. It has to look like we've *never* been here." Panic flooded his voice. "They've probably seen the smoke from our fire. They're coming. We need to leave *now*." Billy started pulling tarps over piles with the hand that wasn't holding the torch. One-handed, he couldn't get them straight.

"Fry, help me!"

While I pulled tarps on top of piles, I began to see Billy's point. How had I overlooked that these were criminals? My heart started to pound in time with my face.

As we left, I saw Billy tuck a five-dollar printing plate under his arm. I was about to say, *Don't you think we should leave* everything *as we found it?*

But Billy slashed at the air with his torch. "Let's go, let's go!"

I ran past him and up the stairs.

Up top, we buckled down: Billy kicked dirt on the fire. I picked up *The Prairie Traveler* and shoved it in my saddlebag. I gathered our kitchen supplies and food, folded up my bed-roll, and went for Long Ears.

Long Ears stamped his left hoof and turned away from me. When I realized he wasn't having any of it, I fished out a sugar cube. His velvety lips scooped it off my palm, and his head didn't turn quite so much as I tried to ease on his bridle. I gave him another.

It became clear that Long Ears knew how to drive a bargain (and I didn't have the time or patience to refuse him). With a sugar cube, I bridled him. With another, I took off his hobble. Sugar cube, put the saddle on his back and tightened the cinches; sugar cube, attached a saddlebag; sugar cube, led Long Ears by the bridle. When I'd finished, only one row of sugar cubes remained in the box.

Storm didn't give Billy the same kind of trouble, so by the time I'd mounted Long Ears, Billy'd swept the whole camp with a leafy branch to cover up our tracks, had found the trail for Old Line Road, and was waiting for me.

Once again, Storm proved to be all the sweetness Long Ears required. Long Ears followed Storm without balking at all. I took no offense. I was glad we were going. I swore I could hear hooves behind us.

The road was truly unused, so we were lucky to have some moonlight to navigate by. A few times it disappeared into undergrowth and Billy dismounted to find the trail on foot. We crossed a dozen or so downed trees and one tiny creek. About every other sound made me jump—branches catching, owls hoo-hooing, a raccoon hustling by.

Even so, I was sapped of strength, and therefore my body went out like a lamp. My one open eyelid—the right—was the first thing to give, becoming leaden. As soon as it closed, the rest of me went limp. So I jerked awake, slept, jerked awake, and slept while riding Long Ears into the night. When I was awake, I'd mumble "Can we stop?" or "How far until we stop?" or "Billy, let's stop."

Billy responded with something like "Try to stay awake, Fry. I know it's been a long, long day . . ." My eye shut by "long, long day," and if he said anything after that, I do not remember it.

Time passed and the trail became a road. Old Miller Road? Possibly. Though I cannot declare it with all certainty because I slept. That is, until Billy guided Storm into the water of a large creek and proceeded to head up the center of it. I opened my right eye as Long Ears' hooves splashed into the water, and woke up absolutely when Long Ears slipped on a moss-covered stone. I grabbed at the saddle horn. For as long as we stayed in that creek, I held on with two hands, wide-awake. It felt like forever, and the change in the sky seemed to prove it. Morning light diluted the dark of night into a yellow pink, then light blue. When sunlight dappled the water, Billy stopped.

I saw a clear patch of land. That's all I remember. I got myself free of the saddle, hobbled Long Ears, and unfurled my bedroll.

I do not remember lying down. I fell asleep that fast.

CHAPTER SEVENTEEN

Hot. It sounded hot. *Ti ti zwee zirre zirre zeee zee,* a bunting sang. High up, leaves brushed one another. The bunting sang again. A squirrel scrabbled up a tree trunk, paused, and gnawed loudly. Katydids and grasshoppers trilled in the grasses, and water trickled over rocks. Again the bunting sang.

I tried to open my eyes. A flash of light. My left eye refused to open, but through my right I made out tree branches edged with sunlight. The sun burned behind the leaves like a white-hot coin. I let my head fall to one side and a pain raced up my neck. I ignored it and stared at a beetle clinging underneath a blade of coneflower. Fluff eddied in the air. Then I became aware of the pulsing heat blanketing my left eye.

I had no idea where I lay. I barely knew my name. The sun's position suggested it was noon or later. I touched my gummed-up left eye and felt hot skin that billowed from cheekbone to eye to nose. I swallowed. My tongue stuck to the roof of my mouth. *Water.*

I sat up. Or *tried* to sit up. In succession, every sore muscle, every bruise, every scrape made itself (and its history) known: a tumble down the rocks at the nowhere place on Miller Road, the fall down pine steps into a cave. Riding all night on the back of a mule hadn't helped things either.

Sometime during that ride, one day had turned into another.

We had been running. Counterfeiters—the lawless—following.

That got me to my feet. I found my canteen in my saddlebag. I unscrewed the top, guzzled water, and looked about me.

Billy slept about twenty feet away under a white pine. His arms were wrapped around his saddle, which he'd used as a pillow. I could hear his breathing, a near snore, coming from under his worn hat. Seemed like he didn't have a care in this world. *He's right,* I told myself. Hadn't we ridden all night long? What people (or person) would follow a man and girl this far?

I remembered I had planned to go back to the Garrows' to ask about that ribbon.

I couldn't do that now. Not if bad men were coming. It would be foolish to even go *toward* Dog Hollow.

Was I sure they were coming for us? Yes. Or I thought so. I *thought* I had heard cracks, pops in the night.

We were in a grove of trees near a large meadow. Several clumps of boulders rose out of the meadow, like the backbone of a sea serpent swimming through the grasses. Long Ears and Storm stood at a far end. They grazed a little, moved a bit, then grazed some more.

The road lay somewhere behind me. We'd ridden up that creek, so we had to be at least an hour's ride off the road. It seemed unlikely that they'd be able to find us.

I couldn't shake the feeling that they were coming.

Think about something else, I thought.

Predictably, I thought about how I'd told Mr. Olmstead, and how that made me the rock that started the landslide.

I would not stew in my thoughts! I needed an escape, a diversion, something to do until Billy woke up and we got moving again. Billy's rifle, the Spencer repeater, lay on the ground next to him. I stared at it for a moment. There might be some amusement in shooting a repeater.

I remembered the bumpy rows of frozen field under my feet, the ice-laced snow shining, the February blue sky. I remembered how, at the edge of the field under a stretch of black oaks, I had seen a band of pigeons. They looked like . . . What had I thought then? Yes—a blue-sky day alighting on earth. The big male had spotted me, twitching his head to see. I had lifted my rifle. I found my target. And everything dropped away, leaving only the big male and me alive together in the world. He saw me. I saw him. We were connected, linked, a wire strung tight between the two of us. *What? What? What?* he thought.

I desperately wanted to go somewhere from *before:* before counterfeiters' caves; before nowhere places; before cougars; before a boxed body that weighed less than two cats. I hadn't appreciated *before* when I'd been there. But now *before* was where I wanted to be, *before* was where I wanted to live.

I laid my hands on Billy's repeating rifle and replaced it with my Springfield single-shot. Then I dug in Billy's saddle-bag for cartridges, grabbed a handful, and decided to follow that creek upstream.

After walking several minutes, I stopped to load the cartridges into the repeater's buttstock, and thought about how guns are easier to understand than people. Every part in a gun has its place and purpose. I took a long look at that Spencer and liked what I saw. Looped below the trigger was a lever. By pushing this lever forward between shots, I'd accomplish three things: First, the used cartridge would fall out of the rifle. Second, a fresh cartridge would be forced into place. And third, the hammer would be cocked. It was a nice mechanism. By my saying this, don't think I preferred a Spencer repeater to my Springfield single-shot. But I can appreciate genuine ingenuity when I see it.

I hoped to utilize that ingenuity too. Three animals lined up—bang, bang, bang—would be just the thing.

But fifteen minutes into my walk I'd seen nothing, not one creature—not a rabbit, not a squirrel. I'd heard birdsong, but I never did figure out the position of those singers. It *was* midday, and everybody knows the world lies a little quieter when the sun beats down. Perhaps I'd made too much noise. I'd been thinking more about *not* thinking than about being silent. But all I wanted was a brute creature to concentrate on and shoot so that I could remember what I'd been like before all of this had happened.

Is that too much to ask?

It was a loud thought. If I'm honest, the thought was directed toward heaven too. Did that make it a prayer? I hadn't prayed once through all of this. Or if I had, it was by accident, mostly in panic. Now I was petitioning for—no, demanding—animals to kill. It didn't seem right, somehow. Not even then.

Anyway, here's the thing I have never forgotten: right after that loud thought-prayer, I heard gunshot. More gunshot. A mule brayed. I *knew* that bray.

My heart jumped like a sparrow in a bush. *Oh no.* Billy was alone. I had his gun. I'd replaced it with my Springfield. Would he be able to use my single-shot effectively and at a second's notice? Probably not. I ran toward Billy, Long Ears, and Storm.

Bolting into a situation makes no sense, particularly with a rifle in hand. I'd end up dead. (I knew that much.) So I slowed to a creep and carefully made my way through the woods to the edge of that meadow.

As I stepped behind a large tree trunk, I heard a deep voice coming from our camp: "Tie him up." The voice sounded familiar. Then I heard: "Where's the girl?"

My heart skidded. They knew about me. It *must* be Mr. Garrow.

Keep moving, I told myself. I went down on my knees and crawled one tree closer. I needed to see our camp so I could figure out what to do.

While I crawled, I appraised my shooting skills. As I'd proved with the cougar, I was no quick draw. My best chance was to hide myself and wait for an opportunity to shoot. This tactic is known as hunting when animals are the target, but it has an altogether different name when man is the object—sharpshooting.

I did not care for that murderous term (though it fit the act). The war with the South had tainted all sharpshooters as those too yellow-bellied to fight man-to-man. But this wasn't a man-to-man fight; this was man-to-girl, and even with the advantage of a repeating rifle, I'd never shot at something that shot back.

I heard Billy's voice. He was speaking loudly. I assumed he did this purposely—in case I could hear him. "She's run off. I couldn't keep her with me."

"She's here," said the deep voice.

Billy spoke again: "I tell you, she ran off in the middle of the night. There's no fixed sense in a girl like that."

I crept to the next tree.

Then I thought I heard a high, raspy voice say something. I couldn't quite make it out. What I heard next was something hard impacting something soft. Billy grunted. My breath rose in my throat and caught like a moth fluttering against a windowpane.

"I said tie him up," came the deep voice. There was a pause. "She's here. That's her mule."

I remembered I'd grabbed a handful of cartridges and loaded them into the Spencer, but how many had I put in? Was it four? Or five? Or six? A Spencer could take seven cartridges. I knew I had *not* completely filled the repeater.

I leaned around a tree trunk and, finally, got a glimpse of our camp. Billy now sat against the pine that he'd been sleeping under. I looked for the Springfield single-shot. I did not see it anywhere, though I'd left it right beside him. In front of Billy and to my right lay the wide, wide meadow with the line of boulders in the center of it.

I watched as a man I'd never seen, a thin man topped with a bowler hat, jerked Billy so he sat closer to the pine, pulled his arms back around the tree trunk, and lashed his wrists together. Then Bowler Hat bound up Billy's legs. The man's bony shoulder blades worked back and forth. When the man finished, Billy looked trussed up like a turkey ready for roasting. Billy hurt too. I couldn't see any blood—at least not at this distance—but I saw him wince with every breath.

I leaned back against the tree. What had I gotten into? I did not want to be here.

Bang!

I *knew* that sound.

I leaned around the edge of the tree for a second time and saw the Springfield—Grandfather Bolte's rifle, *my* rifle—in Bowler Hat's hands. "Should have seen your face. Thought you were dead," he crowed.

Billy hunched lower against the tree trunk.

Bowler Hat strolled up and slapped Billy's face. Billy went white.

"Want to live? Say it. Say you want to live."

Bowler Hat stepped back and waited.

For the joy of it, that man might kill Billy. There had been no one to help Agatha. This time, I was here. I had a gun.

"I want to live," Billy said. I heard fear in his voice.

That settled things. I would do what I could. My conscience would never rest if I left Billy without trying to help.

Then Mr. Garrow—yes, it was indeed him—walked into my sight line. I saw the revolver holstered on his hip and knew I'd only have one shot before I'd be engaged in a shoot-out. As I've mentioned before, I am no quick draw. Once they started shooting, I could not expect to fare well.

Suddenly it became easy to perceive how my sister had ended up shot. Mr. Garrow—the man who could be so neighborly up at his farm (offering water, tin cups, and generous grins)—kept company with Bowler Hat, a man with ice in his veins.

Mr. Garrow was responsible for my sister's untimely demise. I recited the facts that made it so: The pigeoners had come this way. There was the ribbon in the tiny girl's coppery hair. And most damning? Mr. Garrow and Bowler Hat were the *type*. I'd seen everything I needed to see.

They had killed my sister. They were hurting Billy. They'd probably kill Billy too. They *deserved* to die.

Mr. Garrow put a hand on Bowler Hat's shoulder. I heard the word "girl" and realized Mr. Garrow was telling Bowler Hat to find me. I breathed a sigh of relief when Mr. Garrow pointed in a direction well away from where I hid. Bowler Hat left.

I knew if they found me, they would hurt me—like Billy. Or they'd do worse. Like Agatha.

I would shoot before they shot Billy. Or me.

Given the way I've previously described shooting, you may think magic happened here: that the focus came on strong, the world dropping away, and that I knew exactly what to do. But nothing could be further from the truth.

Instead, what happened next was motivated by hate. I report it to you with shame. But so it was. Ugly? Yes. If Mr. Garrow was vile, I had become equally so. And it was through hate's cool dispassion that I evaluated the situation.

Storm and Long Ears had moved to the farthest point in the meadow. *Good,* I thought. At that distance, Long Ears would not come up and nuzzle for sugar cubes. And I saw where I could hide: I would wriggle into that meadow with the line of boulders in the middle. The first set of boulders would serve me well. Billy would be sitting in front of me tied to the pine.

I heard my chance—brass buckles chattering. When I snuck a look, I saw Mr. Garrow had his back to me and was shaking our kitchen pack empty. Pots, pans, cups, and utensils clanked onto the ground. I got on my knees, slipped into the tall grasses of the meadow, and slithered to those boulders. My bruised body felt every inch of that crawl, but I made it.

I was pleased with the location. One of the boulders had cracked open and fallen apart, leaving a wide V that provided an ample view of our camp and plenty of room to move a rifle. But there was a problem: the sunlight would glint off the rifle barrel and give away my location.

What to do? What to do? I needed something to pile on top of the V to shade it. Branches and leaves would be perfect, but I couldn't afford the commotion that would be caused by gathering them. Then I saw my soiled, stiff dark green split skirt.

You may be thinking, *You did not!* Yes I did. If you thought about it levelheadedly, you'd see that I'd wriggled through fresh green grass in a plaid blouse and skirt to get to this boulder. My clothes didn't have grass stains; they had grass *slicks*. Then there was the bruise across the left side of my face, closing up my left eye. (I am sure that bruise had ripened in my sleep.) So I was torn and dirty and bannered with bruises. My hair was surely matted. I'd dispensed with decorum long ago. Wearing bloomers out in the open? If that concerns you, you're splitting hairs.

I pulled off that dark green split skirt and waited for my chance. When Mr. Garrow turned his back again, I slipped the split skirt across the gap in the rock. It left a shady, V-shaped blind with a view into our camp. I stuck the rifle barrel into that blind and snuggled the butt of the gun into my shoulder. I realized I'd had a little luck—I'd bruised my left eye and not my right.

I would have shot Mr. Garrow then, but Bowler Hat made me nervous. The sound of a shot would bring Bowler Hat running from who knows where. If I wanted to survive this, I needed to have both Mr. Garrow and Bowler Hat in sight, so I held my fire.

While I waited for Bowler Hat to return, I succumbed to trepidation. I imagined that Bowler Hat was somewhere behind me. He'd spy me with the rifle, consider me a menace, and shoot me from a distance, a bullet slicing some part of me meant to remain together.

In the meantime, I watched Mr. Garrow methodically paw through our things. He'd finished with the kitchen pack and now shook one of my saddlebags. *The Prairie Traveler* slid out with a thud. Mr. Garrow picked it up, thumbed through it, and tossed it into the embers. The book burst into flame. I felt a jolt of sadness: Captain Randolph Marcy, his itineraries to the West, and my one good guide to journeying—gone. *Even the best-laid plans . . . ,* I thought.

But what best-laid plans covered this? Hadn't I crossed the line where book knowledge helped? It was all me and my wits now.

Mr. Garrow dug in one of Billy's saddlebags. He paused, then slowly pulled out something bricklike—the five-dollar printing plate. Mr. Garrow let the saddlebag drop to the ground.

I knew it! Billy, you idiot!

Mr. Garrow turned his gaze on Billy, strolled over, and kicked him solidly in the ribs—once, twice, three times. Even over Billy's yelps, I heard Billy's rib cage pop. It was the same sound wood makes in a hot, hot fire. Billy went limp. Mr. Garrow stepped over Billy's body, walked back to his horse, and tucked the printing plate into a saddlebag.

I stared at Billy, horrified. I'd held a rifle. I'd *let* him be hurt by that man.

Billy, move! Bile rose in my throat as I realized I could do nothing now.

Then Billy shifted. I gasped with relief.

A high, raspy voice called out: "She's not at the creek."

Bowler Hat. I pulled the rifle into my shoulder. Bowler Hat leaned over Billy. "What you do to him?"

Mr. Garrow ignored his question and pointed out at the meadow—*my* meadow. I distinctly heard: "Go and bring her in." My heart stopped cold.

Through sawing breath, Billy's voice came. He spoke loudly: "Leave her. She's got a rifle—a repeater. She can shoot. She's the best shot in our town."

Bowler Hat jerked around. "You got a mouth. Haven't you had enough?" he said.

"Roy, I told you to do something," said Mr. Garrow sharply.

Bowler Hat glanced out at the meadow. "I'm not going into that meadow if she's got a gun."

"She's a *girl*, Roy." Mr. Garrow walked up to the edge of the meadow and squinted directly at *my* pile of boulders, his right hand over that revolver. I thought about my skirt lying on top of the rocks. Skirts don't look like moss—never have, never will.

I knew what to do. I put my right eye to the sight of the gun and aimed the barrel at Mr. Garrow's chest. As my finger hovered over the trigger, I saw how this would be: I would pull the trigger. One of my cartridges would leave this gun and rip into Mr. Garrow's chest, blood blossoming on his shirt—a blue plaid shirt that looked slate blue from here. *The big male,* I thought. Once again there'd be blue and a rosy red. But this time it would be the blood of a man, and not a pigeon.

He deserved it—he killed Agatha, I thought.

My index finger wrapped around the trigger.

How can you be so sure? It was Agatha's voice singing in my head as clear as any spring cardinal's. It was what she had said on the bright blue February day.

I remembered the look on Mr. Garrow's face upon seeing Agatha's photograph. Now I recognized that look. Mr.

Garrow looked confused. If he'd killed my sister, would he look confused? Mr. Garrow didn't get angry with us either. The only time I'd seen him angry was when he discovered that Billy had taken his five-dollar counterfeiting plate, and then Mr. Garrow showed no hesitation in expressing it. Was I *sure* Mr. Garrow had killed Agatha?

There's no forward or backward from dead, and no breath either. My own thoughts. Earlier. About someone else—a someone else who turned out to be my sister.

And look at all that had happened as a result of Agatha's death. Wouldn't it be the same for the Garrows? If Mr. Garrow died (shot dead by me), there'd be a useful woman without a husband. There'd be no father for at least three children. Maybe Mr. Garrow was lawless. Maybe he did not deserve life. But Agatha was right: Mr. Garrow's living or dying could not be my decision. Why should my bullet be the one that punched his soul from his body and sent it barreling toward some eternal destination?

The thought of eternal destinations made me wonder about myself. Yes, I had given ample thought to the pain involved in dying, where my death might happen, how others would grieve, and what might be said at my funeral. (Who doesn't think such thoughts?) But I had not thought about what would happen to me *after* death. Though I attended church regularly, I'd never been given to religious passions. Agatha was the one who saw God in the natural world, and who prayed with a fervor I found unimaginable. As for me,

I had a hard time understanding how God could distinguish one Georgie Burkhardt from the myriads of thirteen-year-old girls with braided hair, brown eyes, and plain faces. If I had been *sure* that death was only a candle blown out, an endless oblivion as my body broke down and soaked into the earth, I would have found that a comfort. But now I was here—in this meadow with a gun, Billy tied up and hurting, and two bad men in our camp, both armed. In this situation, I found out that deep down I *wondered* if there might be a heaven and a hell and a capital-G someone waiting for me.

Spare me and we'll talk. Please don't let me die.

(I suspect I'm neither the first nor the last that has made bargains with God under trying circumstances.)

I was unsure. My trigger finger went loose. I would not kill. If a mosquito had landed on my neck then, I would have left that insect in peace.

That said, I did not lower the repeater. May I remind you that Billy was still tied to a tree? Roy Bowler Hat had a mean, corroded look. Additionally, Mr. Garrow stood at the edge of the meadow with his eyes glued on the split skirt laid over the top of the rock. His hand hovered like a prairie falcon over the revolver's handle.

Billy said: "She *never* misses."

Shut up, Billy! Shut up, I thought.

Mr. Garrow spun around. "Roy! No!" he said.

Suddenly I saw what Mr. Garrow saw. Bowler Hat swung the butt end of the Springfield rifle—clap, clap, clap—into his palm. He walked to Billy (who was bound to that white pine) and raised the butt end of the Springfield over Billy's head.

I found my mark.

I shot.

I have never heard such a yelp.

I'd known as I took aim that I'd finish the Springfield. I did. The Springfield—*my* Springfield—flew from Bowler Hat's hands, the butt end splintering. Sparks scattered as parts of it landed in the fire and began to burn.

Bowler Hat grabbed at his right hand and hit the ground on his knees, genuflecting up and down, his hands clenched as if in prayer—profane prayer, because he swore up and down the alphabet. "My thumb! My thumb's gone!"

I pushed the lever. A used cartridge dropped and another one moved into its place. I was immediately well aware that I did not know how many cartridges were loaded. I was sure I had three or four, but after that? I did not know. I began to count. *One shot gone.*

Revolver-first, Mr. Garrow stepped into the meadow. I barely heard the bullet that whizzed over my head.

I pointed the rifle barrel at Mr. Garrow.

Remember how I'd placed the split skirt on the V of that cracked boulder? At that moment, the split skirt slid. Yes, it slid off the rock and hit me in the face. Everything—absolutely everything, including Mr. Garrow—disappeared from sight.

I flung the rifle barrel upward—an instinctual act. The split skirt flew up eight, maybe ten feet into the air. I guess Mr. Garrow felt twitchy too. Because from the middle of the meadow, Mr. Garrow twisted and fired one shot into the airborne split skirt. When the bullet hit it, the skirt crumpled into itself, flying farther backward.

While Mr. Garrow was aiming at my skirt, I was aiming at his gun hand.

I shot. Mr. Garrow's revolver made a sound like a cheap dinner bell and flew out of his hand. This caused Mr. Garrow to lose his balance, and he fell into the tall grasses.

I pushed the lever. The used cartridge dropped and a fresh one loaded. *Two shots gone.*

Mr. Garrow spotted his gun in the grass, and scuttled for it on all fours.

I aimed at the ground between Mr. Garrow and that revolver, and pulled the trigger again. *Three shots gone.*

Mr. Garrow leapt backward.

But he made one more attempt to reach for the revolver. That's when I finally stood up from behind that boulder, and I aimed for a spot of ground very near Mr. Garrow's hand.

Mr. Garrow yelled as a bullet ricocheted off the ground in front of him. *Four shots gone.* He jumped up and half skipped toward his horse. "Let's go. We got what we come for," he said to Bowler Hat.

My heart pounded as I pushed the lever. Would there be

another shot? I thought I heard something move into place, but this was not my gun. Its idiosyncrasies were unknown to me.

Bowler Hat was staring at me. "That's no girl," he said. He put his bloody clenched hands on something tucked in the back of his pants. It was the way he reached that made me know it was a pistol. My breath caught in my throat, but I brought my rifle around.

Please, I prayed. I took aim and squeezed the trigger.

The bowler hat popped off his head, revealing his balding pate.

Five shots.

Bowler Hat rubbed his head with his hand, covering his scalp with blood. I was sure he thought some of that blood was from his head, but I was convinced it was from his missing thumb. Anyway, all that blood confused him. He screamed as he ran for his horse. "That is not a girl! That's a hoyden demon!"

I pushed the lever on the repeater and felt nothing move into place. I was certain it was empty now.

My heart leapt to my throat, but I willed myself not to show fear. I did not move. I did not speak. I held the Spencer on them.

From over the rifle barrel, I watched them leave. They left at a gallop.

When they were gone (though dust still hung in the air), I leaned over and vomited. Then I fell on my knees and retched again. I breathed a few unsteady breaths and stood up. When I stopped seeing stars, I ran to Billy.

Billy was bad off. I found my knife and sawed through his bindings. "You shot his *thumb*?" he said.

"I aimed for the gun. Try to get yourself up," I said as I freed his hands. I knew several of his ribs were probably broken, but I needed his help to leave this place.

Hurry, hurry, faster, hurry, I thought. I'd humiliated Mr. Garrow and Bowler Hat. They wouldn't like being bested by a thirteen-year-old girl. (It's not the kind of story one man can tell another.) I did not want to be here upon their return.

I reloaded that Spencer repeater with seven fresh cartridges and kept it nearby while I got us packed.

I prodded the charred and shattered Springfield rifle out of the fire. While there, I spotted *The Prairie Traveler.* All that was left was the spine. I took both because they were mine. I found the blue-green ribbon trampled on the ground. Mr. Garrow had failed to take it with him.

I paused to wonder at Mr. Garrow passing over evidence that suggested he had shot my sister. Why had he been so careless as to leave it behind?

Had he killed my sister? Maybe he hadn't. Mr. Garrow had come after the five-dollar plate. That was all I knew.

I turned around and saw that Billy had gotten upright with the help of the pine, but he lacked the strength to do more than stand. A tall horse like Storm was out of the question, so I put Billy's saddle on Long Ears and walked the mule to him. I hoped he could hoist himself aboard.

One of my last acts was to retrieve my split skirt. I ran through the tall grasses, remembering the Bechtler dollars I'd sewn into the waistband. I found the skirt twisted in some shrubbish wild sunflowers. I tugged it free, and felt for the five bumps in the waistband. The coins were still there. Then I held the skirt up to the sun and found two holes—the bullet had entered through one and exited through the other. I put an index finger in one of them. It was still warm.

Thank you, I thought-prayed as loud as I could.

CHAPTER EIGHTEEN

That afternoon I knew what I needed to do. We needed to leave and Billy needed a doctor. Billy's face had gone putty-colored.

Still, there was a decision to be made. See, Dog Hollow was the closest town. Dog Hollow would have a doctor. And I did not want to go to Dog Hollow. I knew *who else* knew how badly Billy needed a doctor.

I imagined that even reasonable people do not have difficulty recalling the person that cost them a thumb. Forget the vain reasons—*Here comes Four Fingers!*—a thumb is downright useful. Fingers alone? A clamp, not a hand. Additionally, consider how many of us start life sucking our thumbs. Chicken soup doesn't render half the comfort of a thumb. I tell you, people *like* their thumbs. Might as well send an invitation for a personal vendetta. Never mind that it was an accident. I did it. I was a thumb shooter.

I suspected that Mr. Garrow and Bowler Hat would wait for me on the road to Dog Hollow.

Billy and I could head back to Placid, but Placid had to be a journey of at least two days, and two days without a doctor would send Billy to his grave. You don't turn the color of dust unless you're returning to it.

As I saw it, I could choose between death for one of us (Placid) or a good possibility of death for me (Dog Hollow), since I'd be the one holding the gun in the shoot-out. I ask you, what kind of choice is that? Every time I thought the words "Dog Hollow," I shook so badly I could barely hang on to the reins.

In desperation, I recited what I knew: I knew we couldn't stay in the meadow. I also knew I didn't have to decide which way to go until I found Miller Road. At Miller Road, I could choose between east (Dog Hollow) or west (Placid). *Let Miller Road be my crossroads,* I thought.

I was fidgety as we got moving. I'd tethered Long Ears to Storm and told Billy to hold the saddle horn. The repeater lay across my lap. (After that cougar, I did not trust myself to pull it from a holster.) I rode like some sort of ranger, with one hand on the reins, the other hand on the rifle.

I kept glancing back at Billy. He cringed with every one of Long Ears' steps, even though we went slower than I thought wise.

★ ★ ★

The ride that followed goes on and on and on in my mind. It took work to find Miller Road. I did not have a map. I looped some.

Initially, Storm troubled me. I suppose I felt as light as a dried leaf to her. But what I didn't have in weight, I made up for in will. I left little room for misunderstanding and Storm obeyed.

"Tell me one of Agatha's stories," Billy said, speaking for the first time in a while. So I told Agatha's stories: the day the fox kits stole her glove; the story of the kingfisher chasing off a hawk by Cattail Pond. I told him everything I remembered of those last days with Agatha.

Then I told him the story of the old man who was visited by the white pigeon. I told the story fully, spinning it out further than Agatha had done: "As the white pigeon left, the old man peered out after it and saw that the sky was filled with birds. Two of every kind of bird on the whole earth waited for the white pigeon. There were big birds and little birds, long-necked birds and spindly-legged birds, birds with beaks like spoons and others with beaks like tweezers. Those birds came in every color too—green, purple, red, yellow, and orange. When the white pigeon joined them, all the birds flew up . . . up . . . up. Finally, the birds disappeared from sight and the old man stared at an empty blue sky.

"The wise old man stared into that empty sky until the blue turned black, all the while musing about those birds. When the moon came out, the old man got down from his stool, stretched his back, and went to deliver the white pigeon's message. Then he returned home and slept.

"The next day the wise old man stepped outside his forest lodge. He looked up at the sky, remembered the visit by the white pigeon, and was filled with joy. He spread his arms wide and began to spin. He felt like he was flying. He threw back his head and laughed. Then he closed his eyes and spun: spinning, spinning, spinning. He spun until he lost his balance and fell.

"But here was something unexpected: as the man fell, he never struck earth. Instead, he heard whirring. He opened his eyes.

"And what do you think he saw? He saw birds. Birds, birds, birds—a wing, an eye, a beak. They flew so fast he could barely make them out. All around him was a feathered fabric weaving itself in and out. It seemed the birds were lifting him. Or perhaps he'd grown wings? One of his moccasins fell off, and the man watched it fall, seeing for the first time that the earth was far below. That should have scared him, but the wise old man felt no fear. What he felt was the heat of somewhere better warming the top of his head.

"Then a bird called to him. He answered! The birds' language melted on his tongue like honey, and when he spoke it, it felt like laughter. Was he laughing? Or was he calling?"

I stopped there. In front of me passed the Wisconsin River. Normally, I took joy in seeing those slow red waters. But this time I dreaded what came next.

"Won't be long now, Billy. Miller Road has to be around here. Hang on," I said. My heart started to beat furiously.

A minute or two later, I'd found Miller Road. I looked to the east. I looked to the west.

"Billy, tell me what to choose," I whispered. I stared at the road, unable to urge Storm one way or the other.

I turned around in the saddle to look at Billy. Sweat ran down his face as he concentrated on hanging on to that saddle horn. Half dead, partially departed, one foot in this world and one foot in the next—that was Billy from the looks of him.

"Giddap, girl," I said. Come what may, we were going back to Dog Hollow.

"What did you think of my story?" I said loudly to Billy. I said it only because I needed to think of something else besides the danger ahead. I did not expect a response.

But I got one: a thud.

Then: "Ungh."

I turned and saw Billy had slipped off the saddle and fallen to the ground. His right foot was caught up in the stirrup.

"Billy?"

I no longer knew what to do.

I'm sure I do not need to tell you that it didn't seem good that a man with broken ribs had fallen from a mule. I remembered that there was a section on building litters in

The Prairie Traveler, but fire had reduced my guidebook and instruction manual to its spine. So I did what I could: I arranged Billy in a mostly flat manner. Billy sweated, shook, and spoke gibberish.

I had one last choice: to leave or to stay. If I left him to go for help, I imagined either animals or criminals would get him. If I stayed, he'd die—by the side of the road, in a nowhere place.

I would not let him die *alone* in a nowhere place.

So I sat by the side of the road, my ears listening for the hoofbeats of bad men coming, running my fingers up and down that Spencer repeater. I promised myself that when Mr. Garrow and Bowler Hat came, I would shoot until I was dead.

I started to have that talk with God, praying in earnest.

"Listen . . . ," Billy rasped.

"Billy?" There was a clarity in his eyes I hadn't seen an hour earlier.

"Listen to me . . ."

I leaned down, closer. "I can hear," I said.

"I need to tell . . ." His eyes closed.

"I'm here, Billy. I'm here."

"The kiss . . . I *knew* you'd tell . . . I knew you'd see it from your grandfather's study. I *planned* it so you'd see . . . Agatha said good-bye. I made it look . . . more . . . whistled . . ."

I sat back.

Billy opened his eyes and tried unsuccessfully to sit up.

"Lie down," I ordered.

"I'm sorry. I didn't want Agatha to marry Olmstead. Thought Agatha would come back to me if he was gone. She didn't come back. She ran off. I knew then she'd never come back. When she ran off, I asked Polly to marry me."

It had taken everything out of him to say it, cost him strength. He continued: "I *do* love Polly. She would have been ... good wife."

At that moment, I did not care about Polly. I also did not care that he had used the third conditional tense—"would have been"—suggesting the end was in sight.

"You manipulated me?" I said.

He did not answer.

"Used me? Answer me, Billy. If it's the last thing you do, you tell me."

Billy opened his mouth. "Yes ..."

I stood up and looked down at him prone on the ground, so weak—nearly dead, as far as I could tell.

"So, so sorry ... why I came *here*. To make up."

I stared at him for what seemed like a long time. Finally, I said: "You did not show love to my sister. You never cared for me. You talk to your maker about it." And I walked off.

I did not go far.

Furious? Oh yes.

But Billy was dying, for heaven's sake. *Dying*. There is a night-and-day difference between "dying" and "dead."

I turned around, went back, and sat near his head. I told him how it would be (not knowing if he could hear): "My name is Georgina Burkhardt. Miss Burkhardt to you. We are no longer on a first-name basis. In fact, from this day forward, we are strangers."

It was what I imagined Grandfather Bolte would say under such circumstances. How I missed him then! My grandfather always knew what to say, and I imitated him as best I could. I tipped my chin into the air, and I gave Billy a stare as hard as granite. (It did not matter that Billy's eyes were closed as I did it. It made me feel better.)

Then I whispered into Billy's ear: "I'll sit with you, Billy. I won't leave. I'm right here. You are not alone."

Billy's mouth jerked open as if to speak. I leaned in. But all I heard was a hiss, a hard swallow, and "Fry."

I put my head on my knees and started to cry.

Rocks popping under wheels.

Wheels. Not horse hooves.

I ran into the center of the road, waving the hand that didn't hold the repeater. "Stop! Help! Man hurt! Help me, please!" I yelled.

The wagon pulled over to the side. I thought I was hallucinating when I saw Mr. Benjamin Olmstead.

CHAPTER NINETEEN

Next thing I remember is waking in that miraculous room in the American House in Dog Hollow. It wasn't a fancy room. It was slightly larger than a pantry, and held only a bed, a wooden chair, and a mirrored dresser with a bowl and water pitcher set on top. A small square window had been opened for a breeze.

But it was a room without memories. It did not suggest any pasts or futures. It was simply a *room* in a *place* in *time.* The ropes of the bed had been turned tight. The sheets were clean. A rug lay folded at the foot of the bed. In the closet hung a new set of clothes—everything from snow-white bloomers to a fine cloth blouse and, finally, a store-bought split skirt. (Where had Mr. Olmstead found that?)

The miraculous continued when I saw breakfast laid out on a table and, on the floor, a large copper tub for bathing. Every bit of it was paid for by Mr. Olmstead.

I did not remember how I got back to Dog Hollow, or to the inn. I later learned that Mr. Olmstead had traveled with his groundskeeper. Mr. Olmstead had lifted me into the back of the wagon, where I immediately fell asleep. The groundskeeper had found Billy. It took both men to get Billy into the wagon.

Hours later I was rubbing my eyes and pushing off sheets that smelled of sunshine. It seemed to be midmorning, though of what day, I could not say.

I walked to the mirrored dresser. *Is that me?* I thought upon seeing my reflection. The only thing that seemed familiar was my right eye. Then I poured water from the pitcher into the washbasin and splashed it on my face. After drying off, I put my finger on the great bruise and followed its orange and green shoreline as it skimmed around my left eye and lapped against the side of my nose. The deep purple of it lay over my eye and cheekbone. Tentatively I pressed it, watching it lighten and darken. It was tender.

A knock at the door. "You up?" came a voice.

Then, without waiting for my reply, a woman opened the door and walked in.

Unexpected entries no longer suited me. My encounters with bad men (and a certain cougar) had left me skittish. I hopped right into a corner.

"It's all right, kitten. I'm the owner here, Mrs. Tartt," she cooed. She was a storybook character come to life: broomstick-yellow hair, red skirt, blue apron, and green-checked blouse. She held out a hand. I stepped away from the wall but did not come closer.

She put her hand down and said gently: "Mr. Olmstead is right downstairs, sitting on the porch waiting for you. You eat that breakfast. I'll fill this tub with hot water and we'll get you cleaned up. Then you can go downstairs. Mr. Olmstead says you'll be leaving this morning. Billy will be staying with us for a week or so until the doctor says he can travel. Righty-ho?"

Mr. Olmstead is here. Billy is still alive. Relief flooded me.

In twenty minutes, the tub was filled and breakfast proclaimed done, and Mrs. Tartt was scrubbing my body clean. She said she did not trust the job of scrubbing me to anyone but herself. That wasn't the only thing she said either. She kept up a near-constant monologue as she worked over my body with a brush: "My land, these bruises! There's society and savagery, and you sure crossed that line. We've got to bring you back."

You might think I'd be offended, but I wasn't. The warm water felt nice. Mrs. Tartt never scrubbed too hard. And it was clear she didn't expect a response. Her words ran off my back into the water with everything else. When I stepped out of the copper tub and into the towel she held for me, what I'd left behind looked like pond water. I half expected a catfish to surface through the murk for air.

I refused to let her take my old clothes. (She threatened to "burn the whole lot.") After she closed the door, I folded those old clothes gently and tucked them into one of the saddlebags.

I did not meet Mr. Olmstead right away as—yes—I was told to do. See, there was one more question I needed to ask, now that I was back in Dog Hollow. Funny how it was one of the first things Ma had asked me to check when Agatha went missing, and yet I'd been in Dog Hollow two times and had never inquired.

I snuck out a back door of the American House and went to the train station. There were a lot of ifs: *if* Agatha still had her money, *if* she was not injured, *if* she was not forced to run away because the people she traveled with were of questionable quality. But *maybe* my sister had taken the train.

"State your business. I am not here to gossip." The stationmaster's fingers scrambled over small stacks of paper.

He stopped and eyed me.

"I don't gossip," I said.

I got out the photograph of Agatha, slid it under the glass, and said loudly: "Did this young lady buy a ticket from you? It would have been near the end of May. About three weeks ago? She's got the prettiest auburn hair."

"This is a *busy* station. I don't take time to notice facial features and hair coloration," said the man. He pushed the photograph back at me without so much as a glance.

I blocked the passage of the photograph with my hand. "If you haven't seen her, she's *dead*. I'm her sister. *Please* take a look."

The stationmaster frowned, but he took the photograph into his hands and gazed upon it for a lengthy second or two.

He pushed it back under the glass toward me. "There *may* have been a young lady like this. She had a hood over her hair. She left early in the morning."

"Where did she go?"

"I do not know, miss. I barely remember the encounter."

I thought for a moment. "Have you met Darlene Garrow? The young lady that lives up on the bluff with her family?"

He crossed his arms then. "I knew it. Gossip! That's what you came here for, isn't it?"

I did not know what he was talking about, so I pressed on. "*Was* the young lady you saw Darlene Garrow?"

"Are you *implicating* me in all of that?" At this, he picked up a stack of papers again. When I did not budge, he said: "Anything *else* you need? A ticket perhaps?"

"Was this young lady alone or with someone?"

"Gossips!" he said. He drew the shade on his window.

The stationmaster's agitation made no sense until I joined Mr. Olmstead on the porch of the American House.

Mr. Olmstead jumped up as soon as he saw me, and came over. "The men that did this to you will be captured. The sheriff and the federal marshal have recruited a posse to track down Mr. Garrow and his man. The federal marshal has been trying to find a gang of counterfeiters, and it looks like you and Billy found them. He's determined to catch them. The posse left early this morning."

What was Mr. Olmstead talking about? How did he know about the counterfeiters? And what did he mean by "the men that did this to you"? Then part of it dawned on me: "Are you talking about my face?"

"Someone *hit* you."

I sighed. "Everyone seems to deduce that I got hit, but I *fell*. I fell off a big pile of rocks, landed on my cheek, and earned this bruise fair and square. Mr. Garrow and his man are innocent of hurting me. I hurt them. The man traveling with Mr. Garrow? Well, I accidently shot off his thumb." I realized how that sounded, and added: "In defense! He was going to hurt Billy."

Mr. Olmstead's eyes went wide. "You shot off his thumb?"

"With Billy's repeater. I was aiming for the stock of the Springfield and that was where he'd placed his thumb." I saw the look on his face. "It's a long story," I said.

"That's a story I'd like to hear," he said. He chuckled. "Billy told us that there were two of them, and that there was counterfeiting involved. But it was your *face* that made me act." He grinned at me. "Now I see that no one should underestimate Georgie Burkhardt."

"How is Billy?" I said.

"The doctor said he's lucky to be living. Six broken ribs. Some damage to his organs. He'll stay until the doctor says he's rested enough to travel. He's probably awake. Do you want to see him?"

"No sir, sure don't," I said. Even I was surprised how quickly I said it.

Mr. Olmstead smiled sadly. "I take it he told you how he playacted that scene so you'd think Agatha promised him something?"

I nodded.

"He confessed to me too."

I looked into those blue eyes. "I shouldn't have told you."

"No. I should have listened to Agatha when she explained. I was jealous of her relationship with Billy. If I'm honest."

"Thank you for the room and the clothing. Thank you for coming for us," I said.

Mr. Olmstead waved off my gratitude, and indicated that we should sit.

I shook my head. "I'd like to get on my way. I want to go home."

It was true. In my mind, I saw Ma and Grandfather Bolte eating dinner, and I wanted to join them. I smiled slightly, thinking of the pleasure that Grandfather Bolte would get when he heard this story. He'd be angry at first, but Grandfather Bolte never could resist a good story.

"We'll be going soon enough. Please sit, Georgie. I've got news," he said.

It was the way he said it. I sat.

Mr. Olmstead's hand reached out and squeezed mine. "I came because your ma asked me to find you. Your grandfather died two days ago."

"Grandfather Bolte?" I said.

But what other grandfather did I have?

CHAPTER TWENTY

Eventually, there's nothing to be done with a body but bury it.

It was late afternoon when Mr. Olmstead, his grounds-keeper, and I arrived in Placid. Mr. Olmstead had offered a spot in the hotel wagon, but I chose to ride Long Ears.

I would have it no other way. See, Long Ears had stood by me. He had been tried and proven true. All this time he had borne me up. I would not take him for granted like I had done with Grandfather Bolte. *How* could I have missed Grandfather Bolte's last days alive?

I know—how could I have known? Still, I wished I had been with him.

★ ★ ★

As we arrived at Placid's outer boundary, I nudged Long Ears and he broke into that trot. (Yes, it nearly jarred the teeth right out of my head.) We passed the hotel wagon and eased left onto Main Street. That was where I slowed Long Ears to a walk.

Placid was deserted. CLOSED signs hung off doorknobs and in windows. Not one soul sat on a porch. The hoof strikes of our horses and mule echoed eerily off the wooden buildings, and rocks popping from underneath the wagon wheels seemed preternaturally loud. The wind blew a gate. It swung on a squeaky hinge and banged against its fencing.

The Bolte General Store was closed like everything else. On the front steps someone had left a bouquet of black-eyed Susans.

Where was everyone?

I let my eyes trail up the hill that led to Mount Zion Cemetery. I found my town.

According to Mr. Olmstead, Grandfather Bolte fell in front of several customers. His heart gave out, Doc Wilkie said. He died instantaneously.

They waited to hold the funeral as long as they could.

Halfway up the hill, I heard a familiar sound—shoveling. Then in twos, threes, and fours, dark-clad mourners appeared over the lip of the hill. First came a couple wearing black. The man put his cap on. The woman clutched his elbow. More people (women, children, men) began to spill down the hill. I had thought Agatha's funeral was big, but this was bigger. Everyone in Placid must have attended, and plenty from towns one or two over. Long Ears and I parted the mourners, a dark fabric sea of ink black, midnight blue, brown, gray, forest green, burgundy.

The memory came unbidden: Grandfather Bolte saving me from strangulation in that borrowed black dress. I felt his callused fingertips unbuttoning the tiny collar button at the back of my neck. I remembered tightness, then air.

I bit my lip.

Some of the mourners recognized me. "Georgie?" "Georgina, is that you?" "Is that the last Burkhardt girl?" But I averted my eyes, well aware I was a sight with that bruise on my face. I wanted Ma to see me, to find me. No one else.

Then I was at the top of the hill and I saw her. Her back was to me. She was watching people shovel dirt into that hole. One by one, person after person passed the shovel on, then went to take Ma's hand. She wore the same black dress. On her right, where Grandfather Bolte should have been, Sheriff McCabe stood. On her left, where I should have been, a sturdy woman wearing a wide hat of questionable taste had planted herself.

I sat atop Long Ears and observed Ma, unable to urge myself forward. Funny how the last two hundred feet felt insurmountable.

Sheriff McCabe whispered something to Ma. Ma turned. She came running. I had never seen Ma run, but my ma ran. She let nothing stop her, pushing her way through those people (downright shoving one man, who did not see her coming), all to get to me. She wrapped her arms around my waist and pulled me off Long Ears.

Then I stood on the ground and I heard Ma whispering: "One came home! One came home! Georgie, you came home!" She kissed my head, put her hands on my hair, patting me, touching me, kissing my head again. My ears were wet with tears.

"Ma . . . ," I managed.

She held me out from her and ran her fingers over the bruise on my face. "Does it hurt?" she said. But before I could answer, she had gathered me in her arms again.

That was when someone bellowed: "It's about time!" I lifted my head from Ma's shoulder and saw the sturdy woman in the questionable hat.

Ma laughed at the look on my face. "Georgie, this is your aunt Cleo."

A relative? I knew Ma had relations out in upstate New York. She wrote to them faithfully, once a week. But I never thought I'd see one of those upstaters in the flesh. From what I understood, they considered Wisconsin a wilderness devoid of law, manners, and all proper speech. I would have stared further (and eventually issued a greeting), but Ma grabbed hold of me and kissed me again.

As we walked down the hill together—Aunt Cleo with her arm around Ma's waist, Ma holding my hand, me holding

Long Ears' reins—I saw Mr. Olmstead speaking with Sheriff McCabe.

The sheriff stopped talking to watch us. I saw him smiling widely. Then I looked up at Ma and saw that she had met the sheriff's eyes. Like some sort of schoolgirl, she blushed and turned shyly away.

I did not take part in the gathering at our house. "You must be tired," Aunt Cleo said, giving me permission to stay upstairs. From the way she said it, if I had wanted to take part, she would have let me. But I was grateful for the escape. All anyone would want to do was question me.

As the house filled up with sounds—shoes on hardwood, knives and forks tapping on plates, punch glasses chinking, laughter, conversations, and storytelling—I brought the saddlebags into my room.

My room—all *mine* now.

That room had shriveled in the sun. The walls seemed too close. I swore the floor was more worn, the window dirtier, the chair and desk plainer than I remembered. I saw someone had made the bed and tightened the ropes underneath.

I sat down on the chair. I missed Grandfather Bolte as well as Agatha. Further, like an echo, I felt an ache for my pa. *Everyone* was gone. Even those crazy pigeons were gone.

Nothing left. Nothing to be done. No thing, no one, no . . .

I sat for what seemed like two months with those

saddlebags at my feet. Then I got up, dumped the bags out on the bed, and began to sort through them.

There was a knock at the door.

"Georgie?"

It was Ma. She'd come up despite her guests.

I looked at the bed and saw my entire journey—everything from inside my bags—spread out on it.

I opened the door anyway.

The plate she carried made me smile. Ma had piled that plate sky-high with three-berry pie, a thick slice of ham, a currant bun, two cleaned carrots, and a steaming potato stuffed with whipped butter. She set it on the desk and then reached out and squeezed my hand.

I found the photograph of Agatha in the midst of the jumble and handed it to her.

Ma ran her finger around the frame. "I missed seeing her."

"I'm sorry, Ma."

Ma gave me a slight smile and turned her eyes to the items on the bed. She picked up the metal gun barrel from the Springfield and the charred remains of its buttstock. She set them down again without saying a word.

But then she saw the split skirt. She lifted it up, put her finger through a bullet hole, and looked at me. The question was plainly written in her eyes.

"I wasn't wearing it at the time," I said weakly.

Ma's eyes widened further. "Not wearing your skirt . . . ?"

I shook my head.

"Tomorrow I *need* to hear what happened. Today get some rest." Ma embraced me again, and then took a step toward the door.

"Ma?"

She turned back.

"Did Agatha write?"

Ma's eyes went soft. "No, dearest, she didn't."

The weight of those words: a blanket made of lead.

"Oh," I said. I sat down. The ropes under the bed moaned.

Ma may have said something more, but I do not remember. I do not even remember her leaving the room.

Sometime later I compared blue-green cloth. One was a ribbon, the other a piece of fabric from Ma's scrap bag. I placed them next to each other. I looked closely.

The fabric matched—no question in my mind.

I lay back on the bed and stitched together a story: Agatha had been separated from the blue-green gown in some manner. She sold it, or traded it, or had it forcibly taken from her. Somehow, the dress ended up with the Garrow family (a family of less-than-sterling reputation). Then the ribbon had been made, and that ribbon (at least eventually) found its way into the little girl's hair. Since Darlene Garrow was a young lady of Agatha's age with auburn hair, it followed that Darlene Garrow was the one who got shot. Not my sister. Was Darlene wearing the dress when she was shot? It seemed so. *Why* she was wearing it? Who knew?

As for Agatha, if that stationmaster had correctly remembered a young lady traveling by train early in the morning, then that young lady was my sister.

But my sister had not written.

Was she alive?

I did not know.

What had I accomplished by leaving, then? Not much.

"That's a lie," I said out loud.

I had experienced a few things. I'd scared a cougar. I'd learned appreciation for a certain mule. I'd survived a shootout. I'd proposed marriage to Billy, and felt the stab of his betrayal. I remembered the lonesomeness as I sat beside Billy, waiting for his death and then my own. At that moment I'd been whittled down to a paper-thin ache.

Lost to all that knew me. Known to none. Prey for bad men.

The feeling overtook me there and then. (I am haunted by it still at times.)

But then the tattered ends of sounds drifted up from the mourners gathered below. I heard a wave of laughter as one of our neighbors finished his story. Glasses thunked on tabletops. Someone said she'd better help in the kitchen. Another neighbor said she remembered that day . . . and what about the day when . . . ? It was a constant stream of conversations, forks scraping over plates, china jostling. I heard one person comforting another, saying, *There, there, there* . . .

This set me to crying into my pillow. I can't tell you what

that cry was about because there were so many parts. But I can tell you this: I heard the sounds of *my* neighbors. I would be part of them tomorrow.

Then I thought: *I* am *part of them. They* know *I am here.*

I was home.

CHAPTER TWENTY-ONE

Much happened (and quickly) during those first weeks back. I will not detail every last thing, but here are the salient points:

On Saturday, June 17, 1871 (the day of Grandfather Bolte's funeral), the federal marshal and his posse succeeded in capturing what became known as the Garrow Counterfeiting Gang. That week newspaper headlines across the country told of the arrest. Mrs. Hilda Garrow, "the ringleader's wife," was the only member that remained "at large." The newspapers said she had "slipped off without a trace along with her three red-haired children."

I found out later that Mr. Olmstead, the sheriff, and the federal marshal had conspired to keep me out of the newspapers. In the end, it could not be done. "Girl Sharp-shooter Brings Down Counterfeiters" read the headline in the Milwaukee newspaper. I found myself described as "a pigtailed hoyden" with a bruise covering "half her head." In addition, Mr. Garrow called me a "freakishly accurate" sharp-shooter who "shot the thumb off a man at two hundred yards." That wasn't all: I "lay in wait like the snake from the garden of Eden." And in case readers were unclear on the matter, Mr. Garrow concluded: "I've never met a *natural* man who can do such things. This was a daughter of Beelzebub."

I did not deserve that. The only thing I'd done was practice. If you practice, you expect to acquire a modicum of skill.

But with all the ballyhoo, I became notorious. Small children came running into our store, and from half-hidden positions (behind display tables, the front door, even the spittoon) they shot at me with pointed fingers, sticks, and broom handles. Grown men sidled up to tell shooting stories, letting me know I wasn't so much.

The worst part about being notorious, though, was the newspapermen. They arrived during the last week of June. Varmints—every one of them! I hated their darting eyes, their lead-dirtied fingernails, and the timepieces they checked obsessively, pulling them in and out of vest pockets. Those jittery men wanted to know everything about one Georgina Burkhardt. They cornered neighbors, summer visitors, itinerant farmers. Then they slapped open notebooks, fired off questions, and jabbed the air with tiny, dagger-sharp pencils.

Ma sent me to my room and told me to stay there. I happily complied. The onslaught of newspapermen lasted for four days, and I survived it without telling my story.

There was another reason besides the newspapermen's basic repulsiveness for my being less than forthcoming. See, those newspapermen did not want my story in its entirety. They only wanted exaggerated stories of caves full of money and shoot-outs with a girl who claimed kinship with Satan. And *Agatha* was the reason I left! Those newspapermen never asked *one question* about Agatha. That made me mad enough to spit nails.

Counterfeiters? Shoot-outs? Incidental.

I did tell my story, though. I told it to the people who would listen to it all and who knew me well. The second night back, Ma urged me to tell. I did. Seated at the kitchen table, I told Ma, the sheriff (who *again* happened to be there), Mr. Olmstead, and Aunt Cleo. I told them everything I've told you.

I handed them my mementos. They held what remained of the Springfield single-shot and the spine of *The Prairie Traveler*. They put their fingers through the bullet holes in the split skirt. They carefully unwound the ribbon found in the penny-colored hair of a tiny girl. I pointed out that it matched fabric in Ma's sewing basket. I told them what the Dog Hollow stationmaster had said. And then I let them draw their own conclusions.

Apologies were spread around. I said I wished I could

apologize to Agatha (for telling) and to Grandfather Bolte (for spiteful behavior).

"I almost threw him out of the house when I found out what he'd arranged," said Ma.

"I *heard* about that," said Mr. Olmstead.

"I thought you'd never talk to me again," said the sheriff.

Ma pointed at him. "You are a lucky man." She broke into a smile, and the sheriff wrapped his hand around her finger.

Aunt Cleo's eyebrows shifted the minutest bit upward, and finally, I saw it. Good gravy, they'd been friends for so long that I hadn't thought . . .

"Aren't you too old for love?" I said.

Ma grinned, looked at the sheriff, looked at me, and shrugged.

Turned out, while I'd been gone, they'd decided to get married. They weren't wasting any time either. They'd asked Reverend Leland to marry them after the sermon the next week.

I laughed and held up my hands. "Fine. Do as you will," I said.

Did I have any hesitations about my ma and the sheriff? Only one—Billy.

Billy coming home: I dreaded it and wanted it. Mostly, I dreaded it.

But the week after the newspapermen left (the beginning

of July), the sheriff brought Billy home. I watched for him, sure he was around every corner, behind every closed door. But avoidance in Placid is like trying to dodge the wind. Eventually everyone comes upon everyone else.

Five days later it happened. I was by myself that day. The sheriff had enticed Ma out for a picnic (said it'd do her good), and Aunt Cleo was seeing about getting the store roof reshingled in exchange for eradicating a customer's debt.

At that moment, I was searching for something on the shelves under the store counter. I heard the sound of boots and said: "Be right with you." When I straightened up, I found Billy McCabe standing in front of me.

Awkwardness abounded. You can read my face like a book, and Billy did. "I'm not here to cause grief. I've done enough. I know it."

I opened my mouth to speak, but found nothing to say.

"You saved my life. I didn't deserve it. Thank you," he said.

I noticed the dark circles under his eyes, and how he moved tentatively, hunched slightly to the left.

I mumbled something about *everybody* deserving to live.

I meant it. But the way he'd used me pained me still, and I remembered with shame my marriage proposal. I'd had *enough* of Billy McCabe. Though, oddly, I also desired to have a long talk with him. He was the only person who had experienced everything I had.

Overcome with warring emotions, I wished he'd leave.

Billy nodded. "It does you credit that you don't say what you're thinking."

I wondered what *exactly* he thought I was thinking. I could barely read my own mind, so he couldn't be getting the half of it.

Billy rocked on his feet for a moment. Then he stepped forward and laid his hand down on the counter not far from where my own lay. Without thinking, I jerked my hand away.

Billy flinched. "I am so sorry, Georgie."

"Go. *Please,*" I said.

But he didn't go. Instead, he set his eyes on mine. "I consider this a debt of obligation. I hope you'll do me the honor of allowing me to pay you back someday. I won't forget."

I managed to nod, and Billy walked out of our store.

It was the last I saw of Billy McCabe. He kept his *own* distance, because I was by no means avoiding him (nor seeking him out). That summer Billy married Polly Barfod. I did not attend the ceremony, but I heard *all* about it. According to Ma, Billy had tears in his eyes when he said his vows. Polly wiped them gently away with her fingertips. (Ma said all that blond hair elaborately braided around her head made her look like an angel giving a blessing.) Billy shook his head (embarrassed), which tickled Polly. She covered her mouth to stop from laughing, but to no avail. Billy found this funny and snorted into a guffaw. And then the entire place, every last witness sitting in those pews, dissolved into chortling, hooting, and doubled-over laugher. People claim Polly said her vows, but no one heard them (except maybe Billy and Reverend Leland). When the reverend pronounced them man and wife and granted them permission to kiss, Billy and Polly drew together with such devotion that everyone—except the very young—looked away.

They left for Minnesota two days later.

Then there were the last loose ends. For instance, Aunt Cleo decided to stay permanently, proclaiming she craved adventure. She said moving from New York State to the frontier of Wisconsin certainly fit the bill, explaining that people in New York didn't know what a "Wisconsin" was. Ma acquiesced on the condition that she take Grandfather Bolte's room (the biggest in the house).

And after paying my IOU to the store, I bought Long Ears from the sheriff. I'd kept the Bechtler gold dollars because of my yearnings for my pa. But Pa wasn't coming back—like Grandfather Bolte—and I was tired of musing about situations that could never be. So I swapped daydreams for a true friend. The sheriff says he'll never call him Long Ears. But Long Ears knows his name, and so do I.

CHAPTER TWENTY-TWO

Living with uncertainty is like having a rock in your shoe. If you can't remove the rock, you have to figure out how to walk despite it. There is simply no other choice.

I kept busy. Busy helped. Every morning I started early in the store—restocking, sweeping off the porch whether it needed it or not, and straightening displays. When the store opened, I took on tasks that used to be done by Agatha and Grandfather Bolte: I advised customers. I completed the sale by taking money and counting back change. At the end of the day, I gathered up the receipts and went upstairs to record them in the account books on Grandfather Bolte's desk.

I liked it too. "She's got a knack," said Aunt Cleo to Må repeatedly (and in my hearing). Another time Aunt Cleo said that sales ran in the family, and I'd inherited the tendency. I understood what she meant. I felt almost clairvoyant. Sometimes I knew what people wanted or needed before they knew themselves. I certainly liked devising schemes to sell this or that item: I formulated plans. I tweaked wordings on signs and made sure everything looked like a picture postcard from the plate glass window. And despite the circumstances, I felt a kind of congruity with the world and my place in it when the store thrummed like a beehive with Aunt Cleo, Ma, and me each doing our part.

Still, we all wondered about Agatha. At different times, Ma, Aunt Cleo, and the sheriff all asked to see the ribbon again. Mr. Olmstead came by to make me repeat what the Dog Hollow stationmaster had said. I did not offer theories, and no one asked. For the first time, I started to understand what it must have been like for Ma as she wondered about Pa all those years.

I imagine we all came up with ways to deal with the uncertainty. I did two things. First, I wrote letters. I wrote a letter to "The Harrisons, parents of Morgy Harrison, Dog Hollow, Wisconsin." I wrote a letter to "Mrs. Garrow on the bluff, Dog Hollow, Wisconsin" and enclosed a piece of the blue-green ribbon. Then I wrote a letter to the University of Wisconsin at Madison. The address read: "The Department That Educates Young Ladies in the Sciences." It was an unlikely address, but I had to try. "If you see her, tell her to write us. We are longing for a word."

Second, I arose one morning while it was still dark, saddled Long Ears, and rode to the bluffs.

Agatha had not come home, so I found a wide rock that overlooked the Wisconsin River and spoke about her loudly into the wind. I told her story. I told my story. I apologized.

Agatha had not come home, so I told the air, the sky, the horizon (and, I suppose, Long Ears) what Agatha looked like when, parasol in hand, she spun under pigeons: spring set free, a dance of heaven and earth, mankind and creation enjoying each other's company.

Agatha had not come home, so I stood at the edge of that bluff, pulled up a dandelion gone white with seeds, and blew those seeds into the wind. I watched them sail off, tottering, turning, and gradually descending to the river below.

And I swear I saw a single blue feather in the wind.

I watched it and remembered shooting those gin bottles after Agatha's funeral. Feathers had flown up with every shattering. I had wondered about the difference between feathers and leaves, and now my thoughts came back to me. It was too true: Agatha had been carried away, beyond my reach, like some sort of feather. Me? I'd had my flight and was back at home. I found I did not mind.

I could have gone on, but Long Ears nudged in to check my pockets for sugar, found none there, and tipped me over.

I pushed his muzzle off me, stood up, and noticed the perfection of the day—not a cloud in the sky, not a breeze. And there was that mule with the ears that stuck out like hands on a clock, eyeing me.

I love it when he waits like that. Long Ears knows it.

I smiled at him, then looked again out over the edge of the bluff.

Yes, I'd said what I needed to say.

Long Ears stamped.

I turned to him, and laughed for the first time that day. "What about an apple? Would that do?"

CHAPTER TWENTY-THREE

On July 24, 1871, Ma shuffled through the mail (like she did). She squinted at the return address on a letter. A small sound—her tongue clicking—escaped her lips. The letter slipped from her hand.

I watched it slice through the air like a feather and I *knew*.

I *knew* before it hit the ground and skidded across the pine floor.

Aunt Cleo hurried to pick it up. I watched Aunt Cleo's face open up like the letter *O*.

Ma set the rest of the mail down and grabbed the letter from Aunt Cleo's hand. Aunt Cleo shooed a customer out of the store and flipped the OPEN sign to CLOSED. Ma ripped the envelope off the letter. A newspaper clipping flapped to the ground. I picked up the clipping, and ran behind Ma to read over her shoulder.

We read the letter together:

Dearest Ones,

Let me tell you that I am fine, since I am sure you are worried. I am in Madison, staying at a reputable boardinghouse for lady students. I've got a job as a store clerk. All is well, except for the turmoil in my thoughts and heart.

First, let me ask about the newspaper clipping. Georgie, tell me this is not about you! The sketch makes you seem quite transformed. I think you must have gone to Dog Hollow to find me. What have I done? I can barely sleep for worry.

I unfolded the newspaper clipping and saw the headline: "Girl Sharpshooter Brings Down Counterfeiters." The sketch beneath it was also familiar, but it never ceased to cool my blood. Below perfectly fine pigtails wasn't a head but a chunk of meat gone bad in the sun. I touched my cheek reflexively.

Aunt Cleo snatched the clipping out of my hands. "You *never* looked like *that.*"

We continued to read the letter:

I was upset when Benjamin broke off our engagement, and stubbornly determined to leave at once in order to study at a university. I decided to slip off and to avoid contacting

231

you until I'd started my studies. I thought if my education was well under way that <u>even you</u>, Grandfather, might let me stay.

I made a hasty decision to leave with pigeoners traveling to Prairie du Chien. At the time, I had a vague idea about attending a university in Iowa or Minnesota—too true that my thoughts were scattered. Mostly, I wanted to leave Placid as quickly as possible.

Soon after leaving, however, I began to suspect that the pigeoners I traveled with were untrustworthy. So in order to avoid any trouble, I separated myself from them at my first opportunity.

That opportunity came at Dog Hollow, when the pigeoners met up with a Mr. Garrow. (The same Garrow as in the clipping?) He wanted to conduct his business in private, so I walked into town with his daughter Darlene. As the two of us talked, Darlene revealed she was engaged but had no wedding dress.

Ma, I sold her the ball gown. I am sorry not to have it, but Darlene was thrilled. What better use for such a beautiful dress than as a wedding dress? The color looked <u>so</u> well on her (her hair is the same color as mine). Though I ache over the loss of your handiwork, I am to be a student, and will spend my spare time studying. My heart is broken. I cannot imagine attending balls and assemblies.

Anyway, Darlene promised not to tell the pigeoners where I'd gone. I spent that night in the woods, and the next morning I boarded the first train leaving Dog Hollow. Because I had not traveled as far as I thought I would, it *made perfect sense to turn around and go to Madison. I also thought doubling back might throw you off my trail. So here I am in Madison.*

Grandfather, you are correct in saying that the University of Wisconsin doesn't educate women in the way that they should. But I've found people here who have promised to help me learn all that I can.

Ma, please show this letter to Mr. Olmstead. Please tell him how sorry I am for my behavior.

All of you—please write. Write that you are alive and well. Tell me what happened. Those newspaper articles scared me nearly to <u>death</u>. You can write to the address below.

All my love (such as it is),
Agatha

"Heedless girl," said Aunt Cleo.

"She doesn't know the half of it," said Ma.

I stood slack-jawed. Then I rammed my knee hard into the counter. "I hate her. She deceived us," I said.

The store went quiet as a hairpin. I looked up and saw their wide eyes staring at me. I read concern—for *me*.

Even after all I'd done—leaving and making my family sick with worry.

After all that, Ma, Aunt Cleo, the sheriff, Mr. Olmstead, our neighbors, all of Placid had taken me back in a most unreserved way.

Wouldn't I do the same for Agatha?

I saw the letter held between Ma's index finger and thumb. I reached for it. I spread it flat on the counter. Agatha's handwriting. Those loopy letter *e*'s. I put my finger on the inked letters and pressed against the lines, feeling every indent as if it were braille.

I *wanted* my sister. I *loved* my sister.

I did it then—I forgave her . . .

. . . and burst out laughing (confusing Ma and Aunt Cleo to no end). I laughed at the irony: Agatha and I had both started in Placid and ended in Dog Hollow. Yet who would say we'd had the same journey? It was as if I had walked, tilling the earth for troubles, and Agatha had bypassed it all by flying overhead.

Agatha was alive.

Ma reached out for Aunt Cleo and me. With our arms around each other, we smiled until it hurt.

Pause a moment. Feel the air surround that moment. Push against it, and find that it truly exists. Blow on it, and see how the tiny barbs snag the wind and lift. Watch it fly.

Feather by feather, she *had* made her way.

CHAPTER TWENTY-FOUR

You'd think 1871 would have finished with me. This was not the case. There are still a few wonders I need to relay before I end my story. The year 1871 seemed determined to remake me, and it did. In the end, 1871 remade *all* of us.

As letters went back and forth, 1871 established itself firmly as a year we'd never be able to forget. Already we'd experienced the largest pigeon nesting within recorded memory, and now in August talk was all about lack of rain. People complained of low water levels in their wells, and of slogging pails of water to their gardens. When had it last rained? I remembered big drops the day I'd negotiated with Billy McCabe for a horse. But after that, everything went bone-dry.

Of course, everyone in my family (including myself) was happily preoccupied with Agatha. We scribbled out missives and eagerly awaited replies. Ma and the sheriff made plans for a November honeymoon to Madison. At Agatha's request, they invited Mr. Olmstead to join them.

By September 1871, though, the drought was impossible to ignore. By then, the news was that all of the Middle West was afflicted. In Placid, a smell like burnt toast coated the wind, the air tasted stale, and a brown haze rested on the horizon. A few days later, the haze migrated into town, and people found it cradled in cupboards and washbasins. The *Placid Independent* reported odd fires in the north (Minnesota, northeastern Wisconsin), which caused people to question the sanity of the editor. Ground so hot it burned holes in people's shoes? Wisps of fire streaking through the forest like fairies? Without a doubt, though, fire threatened. We kept about our business with pails of water at the ready.

Out of this brown haze came a knock at the door. I heard Ma and Aunt Cleo speaking with a woman in the front hallway. The woman coughed. Ma said something about the smoke.

Then I heard: "I could use a guide."

"That's no trouble. I'll take you," Ma said.

It sounded like another person had come to see Grandfather Bolte's grave. All summer we'd been taking people up to Mount Zion Cemetery so they could say their good-byes.

But some quality in that voice made me curious. I cleaned

my hands of the bread I kneaded and stepped into the back garden to see who'd come.

What I saw was a boy-sized woman with straight hips and a purposeful walk—a useful woman—striding straight up the hill to Mount Zion Cemetery. That walk brought back a terraced farm on the back of a bluff—Mrs. Garrow. She walked with such quick steps Ma could not keep up.

I remembered that Ma had never met Mrs. Garrow. I grabbed my coat and raced after them.

I caught up as Ma's hand flitted out in the direction of the marker:

GEORGE LEWIS BOLTE
HUSBAND, FATHER, FRIEND
1789—1871

Mrs. Garrow read the name and frowned. "Where is it?"

I stepped up, startling Ma, and pointed. "The grave bearing my sister's name is there."

Mrs. Garrow stepped hastily over to the tombstone. "Agatha Burkhardt?"

I nodded.

Like that, Mrs. Garrow sat down in front of the tombstone. Then she scooted forward to lay her hands on the letters.

A small sound left Ma's lips. Then she said: "Are *you* Mrs. Garrow?"

Mrs. Garrow nodded, her eyes never leaving the tombstone. She ran her hands down each side of its curve. Then she leaned her forehead against the tombstone and slammed the ground with a closed fist.

Ma sat down and wrapped her arms around Mrs. Garrow. In the dim light of that smoky September afternoon, Ma and Mrs. Garrow sat for some time.

It was an accident. Three days after she got the dress from Agatha, Darlene met Morgy Harrison up Old Line Road at a wide, grassy spot with purple-gray boulders. From that location, a person saw the Wisconsin River winding its way below, and the rocky bluffs beyond, scruffy with pine, hemlock, and oak. It was a romantic place tucked in the bluffs. Darlene knew it well because this spot hid her father's cave.

At the sound of Morgy's horse, Darlene stepped out in the open so the first thing he'd see was her in that ball gown. It did the trick. Morgy gasped. The afternoon sun seemed to set sparks of fire racing through her russet hair. And that dress! It was a living deep blue-green interwoven with hints of color (midnight, robin-egg blue, evergreen, gold) that surfaced and submerged as Darlene twirled and twirled. That day Darlene seemed like some sort of divine being to Morgy. When he met her eyes, she grinned, pleased with his response.

But then Mr. Garrow walked into the clearing with packs full of his "business" (as they called it). Darlene hadn't expected him.

As soon as he laid eyes on Darlene, Mr. Garrow's face purpled.

He set his rifle down, placed his packs beside it, and began to yell at Darlene. Morgy couldn't hear it all, but he thought he heard something about "lying about that girl."

"How do you think that made me look?" Mr. Garrow said several times. He began to circle Darlene.

Darlene could give as good as she got. She yelled back and began to walk. They circled each other.

Morgy hopped off his horse and ran to split the two of them up. Darlene twisted free of his grip and shoved him aside. Morgy decided to let them go at it. He knew they were both hotheaded, but that they loved one another.

It might have all turned out well, except that Mr. Garrow caught hold of that dress. In his grasp, a section of the skirt ripped free.

Darlene became still. She ran her hand slowly over the rip.

"You can repair that," Mr. Garrow said weakly. He offered up the fabric.

Darlene slapped his hand away. "I am sick to death of you and Ma telling me what I can and cannot do." Darlene walked over to her father's packs and reached for the rifle.

And this is an important fact: The packs had shifted. They'd rolled over the rifle. Now the rifle lay barrel out, under the packs. Darlene put her hand on the barrel. "I am leaving with Morgy today. You can't stop us."

"It's loaded . . . ," Mr. Garrow yelled.

It is unwise to pull a gun by its barrel, but Darlene pulled. When the gun stuck, she wrapped both hands around the barrel and tugged harder.

The gun went off.

In the next moment, Mr. Garrow gathered Darlene up in his arms.

"That's what Morgy told me. My husband doted on that girl. Called her his darling," Mrs. Garrow said as she stood.

Ma got up with Mrs. Garrow and gave her a handkerchief. Mrs. Garrow used it and continued: "My husband, Blair, made Morgy leave, told him to write a note to his family saying he'd eloped, and gave Morgy a tidy sum to do it too. I know Blair was scared of telling me. *I'm* the one thing he *is* afraid of. That fool! I'd half forgive him for the accident if he had only buried her right off. He panicked— that's all I can think. Leaving her where animals could get at her!"

"But how did that body come to be on Miller Road?" I said.

Mrs. Garrow shook her head. "How am I to know? I can't ask. If I go near my husband, I'll get arrested myself. I've got three children."

"Don't you have a theory? Anything?" I said.

Mrs. Garrow shrugged. "He might have left her on Miller Road because it's well traveled. Maybe he figured someone would see the red hair and bring the body back to us—we're the only family with red hair. It would look like an accident, and I would never know he had anything to do with it. Morgy would be another matter, but Blair knows how to deal with that sort of situation. It's me he can't figure out."

I crossed my arms. "But *our* sheriff found that body."

"Coincidence," she said in a tone that suggested absolute confidence.

Ma said: "I *made* that dress, though. That's *two* coincidences. There's *three* if you count the similarity between the girls."

Mrs. Garrow took this in.

Suddenly her face cracked into a wide grin. "Ha! You think my Blair is *that* clever? You've got a high opinion of the malefactor's mind!" Mrs. Garrow coughed, and the cough became a scratchy, bone-rattling laugh.

Then Mrs. Garrow met my eyes. "Mrs. Harrison and I got your letters. We figured my visit would be enough of an answer."

I said it was.

As Mrs. Garrow left, she pressed a wad of banknotes into Ma's hand for a revised tombstone. We watched her disappear into the brown haze, and then Ma looked down at the bills in her hand. "Do I dare use these?" she said.

The money *was* counterfeit. Despite this, a new tombstone appeared in the cemetery where Agatha's used to stand. The inscription was simple:

?—1871

DARLENE GARROW

CALLED DARLING

Ma never said a word, but I'm sure she arranged for the tombstone. Agatha's tombstone appeared in the root cellar, words to the wall. Waste not, want not, Ma always says.

A story cannot end where there's smoke, and where there was smoke in 1871, there came Sunday, October 8.

Remember? That was the day an inferno blazed along the shores of Lake Michigan. Every issue of the *Placid Independent* that fall (and into the winter) brought news of the Great Chicago Fire. Didn't we all pore over newspaper pages filled with illustrations of swarms of people pushing over bridges, or of fire pluming from sinking ships on Lake Michigan and billowing from tall, tall buildings onshore? I still see the one of two girls with eyes round as plums hovering over a third girl who lay still. The numbers of Chicago homeless crept up with every report, until finally I read somewhere that one hundred thousand people were without a home.

What you didn't hear about was the *second* fire. Yes, there were *two* distinct fires that night—one down in Chicago, and the other up along the shores of Lake Michigan in Wisconsin. As it turned out, more people died in the Wisconsin fires. We in Placid knew all about this fire because the survivors appeared at our borders.

And so began the second great migration of 1871. This time the migration was all earthbound. The survivors came, carried by oxen, horses, or wagons, or on their own two feet. They spoke of a fire so hot it split boulders, melted metal, and wrapped trees in glass. They said those that survived had run into Lake Michigan to escape the fire. When they walked out of the lake the next morning, there were no landmarks to guide them. They did not know where they stood. They saw only miles and miles of blackened beach.

For months, our doctor was so busy with the burned that he slept in two-hour increments. Every extra space in Placid, Wisconsin, was filled: parlors became bedrooms, an empty stall became a home. A shed on Main Street that had been used to prepare and barrel pigeons had three people living in it (a small boy, an uncle, a cousin). People slept between the pews at the churches. The town hall became a makeshift one-night hotel for those needing a place to bed down before journeying on. The inns let survivors stay for free as long as the room wasn't already booked. The Olmstead Hotel donated an entire floor to the cause. Ten people stayed in our home at various times: a girl and her mother, three farmers, two sisters, an elderly woman, a midwife, and a butcher.

For most of these survivors, Placid, Wisconsin, was only a pass-through space, not a settling place. Still, a few survivors decided to stay in Placid. They saw that their skills filled a need. Or they made friends and wanted to continue the conversation. Or they fell in love. Yes, even knee-scuffing, will-you-marry-me love happened. I tell you, near anything can come from ashes.

It's too true that some survivors never got a chance to think of rebuilding their lives. These people breathed their last in temporary beds. We dug them graves at Mount Zion Cemetery, put their names (if they'd been able to tell them) on markers, and paid them the respects we were able.

Every once in a while, I rode Long Ears up to the cemetery and laid flowers on those graves. I tried to remember each person's particulars (a walk, a smile, the way they clung to a photograph). I spoke the names I knew.

"You are not in nowhere," I told the dead.

The ones that lingered in our town, I befriended—if they'd have me. (A notorious thirteen-year-old thumb shooter isn't to everyone's taste.) I listened to their stories. I told my own. Some of them wished they'd passed away with their families. Some of them felt surviving meant God wanted them to do something remarkable. Whatever they thought, I wanted them to know that this small corner of Wisconsin would make a fine home.

As I did this, I thought of Ma, Aunt Cleo, the sheriff, Mr. Olmstead, and our friends and neighbors in Placid. For the most part, they'd let me back into their hearts unconditionally. I tell you, it felt good to give to others what I'd received myself.

I suppose you're wondering, so I'll say it: I have laid down my gun. In the end, there is nothing else for it. I speak here metaphorically because, as you know, the Springfield single-shot is in pieces. But I haven't hunted since all this happened, and I don't expect to hunt in the future. Truth be told, I do not find taking life—*any* life—palatable anymore. I'm well aware that it was *life* I was taking.

Nothing is a "target" anymore. Nothing is "*just* one bird."

Nor is there any satisfaction to be had in one *less* anything—not one less father, not one less grandfather, not one less sister. Not one less cougar (though I wouldn't mind them keeping their distance). Likewise, not one less Mr. Garrow or Bowler Hat. And not even one less fire survivor, even though they've taken over the parlor until all of kingdom come.

I do not even think an animal as abundant as the wild pigeon should be minus one. I say let all the earth be alive and overwhelmingly so. Let the sky be pressed to bursting with wings, beaks, pumping hearts, and driving muscles. Let it be noisy. Let it make a mess. Then let me find my allotted space. Let me feel how I bump up against every other living thing on this earth. Let me learn to spin.

AUTHOR'S NOTE

One Came Home is a work of fiction set in 1871 in south-central Wisconsin. There are a host of questions held in that simple statement. "What's the truth?" and "What's made up?" only scratch the surface. I'm fairly certain that all authors write historical fiction in their own way, so I'd like to describe a few of the ways I've used history in this story.

The Passenger Pigeons

I began writing this story after reading a history of passenger pigeons (A. W. Schorger's *The Passenger Pigeon*). Therefore, it seems right to start with the birds that guided my passage through 1871 Wisconsin.

Commonly called wild pigeons, passenger pigeons were once so abundant on the North American continent that people did not even try to number them. Millions? Billions? No one knows for certain. Observers used words like "countless," "great numbers," and "infinite." The pigeons flew in huge flocks that struck fear, wonder, and party-like giddiness in spectators. But the birds that seemed infinite were proven finite when, in 1914, the last captive bird, named Martha, died at the Cincinnati Zoo. And so the tale of the passenger pigeon became one of the great extinction stories of our time.

I recommend researching it for yourself. You'll marvel. I did. I often raced off to find my husband, book in hand, to read some passage aloud. In the end, I decided these accounts sounded a lot more like science fiction than something from our not-so-distant past. Perhaps you'll have similar feelings.

I do want to issue a warning, though. In the early source material, there is much misinformation about passenger pigeons, particularly about their habits (for instance, how many eggs they laid or how many nests they produced during mating season). A. W. Schorger spent twenty years (at least) researching passenger pigeons. He combed through over two thousand books and over ten thousand local newspapers, and he conducted interviews through correspondence and in person with people who had seen the pigeons firsthand. (Schorger did this work from the 1930s to the 1950s, long before the Internet might have helped him. It was a big job.) In 1955, he finally published his history. He wrote this in the preface to *The Passenger Pigeon:*

> It is unfortunate and most regrettable that no
> competent ornithologist attempted to make a
> comprehensive study of the nesting and other

phases of the life history of the passenger pigeon while it existed in large numbers. Writers from Wilson to Brewster recorded largely what they were told by local residents and trappers. Many of the statements are inaccurate, but they appear repeatedly.... It is not an easy task to reconstruct the life history of an extinct species in the face of a large and contradictory literature since much is beyond absolute proof. The reader may not agree with some of the conclusions, but these have been reached after much sifting and reasoning.

As they say, forewarned is forearmed. This is good information for readers and writers alike! In the end, I decided to use Schorger's history as my primary guide. Though I read secondary source material published more recently, I found none of it as helpful as Schorger's book. That said, I take full responsibility for any mistakes I may have made in this fictional rendering.

What part of the passenger-pigeon history relates specifically to my story? In 1871, the largest nesting of pigeons ever recorded occurred in south-central Wisconsin. The width of the nesting was between six and ten miles, and the entire length was 125 miles. It was shaped like a capital *L*. The short end went up north at least fifty-five miles. The long end finished seventy miles later. This was an *extremely* large nesting.

Schorger estimates that an *average* passenger-pigeon nesting would have been about three miles wide and ten miles long, or thirty square miles. As for the 1871 nesting, Schorger gives a "conservative estimate" of 850 square miles. He also suggests that perhaps *all* the passenger pigeons in North America were in this nesting.

Reading this stunned me. Wisconsin is *my* state—where I grew up—and as far as I knew, our fame lay in cows, cheddar cheese, and rogue cheese curds (illegal in several states), whose authenticity was verified by the squeak they made as you ate them. Why had no one told me about all these birds and this last great nesting?

Maybe they did. Some things are only heard when a person is ready to hear them. When, several days later, this 1871 nesting was still knocking about in my head, I knew I had to roll up my sleeves and write. That was the beginning of this book.

As it turned out, I used the passenger pigeons and the 1871 nesting as a living, breathing setting for this story. I did my best to keep to known behaviors of the passenger pigeons (according to Schorger). I figured there was nothing to be gained by publishing *more* inaccurate information about passenger pigeons. This is despite the fact that people in 1871 would have often thought these inaccuracies true.

In addition, the way I've depicted the human response to the passenger pigeons has some basis in a historical account, though not specific to the 1871 nesting. I couldn't find enough material from 1871 to construct the reality of one particular town experiencing that migration. So I decided to use any account I found within the historical record to create scenes between people and wild pigeons. Since 1871 was the year of the largest nesting ever recorded (with possibly every passenger pigeon present), my description seemed at least plausible to me.

What of Agatha, parasol in hand, spinning under the pigeons? I made it up using this recorded observation: in flight, passenger pigeons had the habit of *exactly* following the path of the bird in front of them. John James Audubon, the famous naturalist, told of seeing a hawk attacking a line of pigeons. The first pigeon dove to escape the hawk, and Audubon said that the subsequent birds all dove in the exact same path, for a long time, even though the hawk had left.

In my imagination, this odd fact combined with what I knew of my character Agatha. She'd be captivated by one bird following another so exactly. I could see an experiment (as well as a game) forming in her mind. She'd want to see what would happen if she slowly pushed something—such as a parasol—in the birds' flight path. When the birds altered their path and flew around her? Agatha would be delighted and, yes, she'd spin.

In reality, would the passenger pigeons have adjusted to a parasol? I have no idea—I wish there were a way to find out—but I loved the image and kept it. (By the way, both of the Audubon books mentioned in the story are books you can read for yourself: *Birds of America* and *Ornithological Biography*.)

Randolph B. Marcy's *The Prairie Traveler: A Hand-Book for Overland Expeditions*

This book actually existed in 1871, and I quote directly from its pages. It's available on Google Books, so feel free to check it out. It combines helpful information (routes, packing lists, recipes) with stories from Marcy's travels. For the most part, I found his advice and writing delightful. Yet take heed: Marcy is a writer from the nineteenth century, and his sometimes shocking prejudices are preserved along with his prose.

Placid, Wisconsin (and Other Places in the Book)

Placid does have a location on the map. It is approximately where the city of Wisconsin Dells is currently located, and it shares its geographic details. I chose to call the town Placid because I wanted the freedom to imagine this town completely. Dog Hollow, with its Smoke River, is completely fictional, and named after a road I found on a Wisconsin map. (It put me in mind of a lone dog—perhaps a beagle—yowling in a tiny valley, and I could not forget the name.) Prairie du Chien existed in 1871 and still exists today at the junction of the Wisconsin and Mississippi rivers. No one could ask for a lovelier location.

The Firestorms

On October 8, 1871, both the city of Chicago and many small lumber towns along the Wisconsin shoreline of Lake Michigan experienced huge firestorms. Afterward, survivors of the Wisconsin fire wandered from town to town seeking medical help. I doubt that survivors would have wandered as far inland as Placid. I chose to imagine it, though, because I was struck by the huge outpouring of compassion they received. As the survivors arrived (and word finally got out), small towns across the state—made up of one ordinary citizen after the next—took strangers into their homes and cared for them.

More at AmyTimberlake.com

I'll be posting more thoughts on my writing process, and other supplementary material, on my website, so feel free to amble about. Enjoy yourself!

SELECTED SOURCES

(ALL OF THESE SOURCES ARE INTENDED FOR THE ADULT READER.)

Audubon, John James. *Birds of America.* web4.audubon.org /bird/BoA/BOA_index.html.

———. *Ornithological Biography.* Philadelphia, 1832.

Bonta, Marcia Myers. *Women in the Field: America's Pioneering Women Naturalists.* College Station: Texas A&M University Press, 1991.

Cokinos, Christopher. *Hope Is the Thing with Feathers: A Personal Chronicle of Vanished Birds.* New York: Tarcher/Putnam, 2000.

Eckert, Allan W. *The Silent Sky: The Incredible Extinction of the Passenger Pigeon.* Lincoln, Neb.: iUniverse.com, 2000. First published 1965 by Little, Brown.

Faust, Drew Gilpin. *This Republic of Suffering: Death and the American Civil War.* New York: Alfred A. Knopf, 2008.

Gess, Denise, and William Lutz. *Firestorm at Peshtigo: A Town, Its People, and the Deadliest Fire in American History.* New York: Henry Holt, 2002.

Marcy, Randolph B. *The Prairie Traveler: A Hand-Book for Overland Expeditions.* Bedford, Mass.: Applewood Books, 1993.

Muir, John. "The Story of My Boyhood and Youth." In *Muir Nature Writing.* New York: Library of America, 1997.

Price, Jennifer. *Flight Maps: Adventures with Nature in Modern America.* New York: Basic Books, 1999.

Rath, Sara. *Pioneer Photographer: Wisconsin's H. H. Bennett.* Madison, Wisc.: Tamarack Press, 1979.

Schorger, A. W. "The Great Wisconsin Passenger Pigeon Nesting of 1871." *Proceedings of the Linnaean Society of New York* 48 (October 1937):1–26.

―――. *The Passenger Pigeon: Its Natural History and Extinction.* Norman: University of Oklahoma Press, 1955.

Wisconsin Historical Society. wisconsinhistory.org.

ACKNOWLEDGMENTS

Without A. W. Schorger's excellent *The Passenger Pigeon,* this novel would not have been written. I also quote from Randolph B. Marcy's *The Prairie Traveler.* I am indebted to both of these authors. In addition, I am grateful to Hedgebrook for granting me a residency in 2009. Furthermore, Elizabeth Fama, Kate Hannigan Issa, Linda Kimball, Carol Fisher Saller, my Bible study group, and my church have all provided significant support. Thank you to Knopf, and my insightful and ever-hopeful editor, Allison Wortche. Thanks also to my agent, Steven Malk, who has been crucial in guiding this book to publication. My family knows only too well how long it takes to write a book since writing is time away from them, so I thank them especially. And finally, I'd like to remember my father, James K. Richardson Jr., who died in 2009, as I was drafting this book. A creative man himself, he loved that I wrote stories. I wish he could read this one.

ABOUT THE AUTHOR

Amy Timberlake is an amateur birder, a farmers' market enthusiast, and a writer. She currently lives in the big city of Chicago, but grew up in a small town in Wisconsin. She remains convinced that the *best* stories take place in the Midwest. She is the author of *That Girl Lucy Moon* (a Book Sense Pick) and *The Dirty Cowboy* (winner of the Golden Kite Award and a finalist for the Western Writers of America Spur Award). For more information—or perhaps to say hello—go to her website at AmyTimberlake.com.